Ravish

Ravish

The Awakening of Sleeping Beauty

Cathy Yardley

red

AVON

An Imprint of HarperCollinsPublishers

HarperCollins books may be purchased for educational, business, or sales promotional use. For information please write: Special Markets Department, HarperCollins Publishers, 10 East 53rd Street, New York, NY 10022.

FIRST AVON RED PAPERBACK EDITION PUBLISHED 2008, REISSUED 2013.

Designed by Diahann Sturge

The Library of Congress has cataloged the original paperback edition as follows:
Yardley, Cathy.
    Ravish: the awakening of sleeping beauty / Cathy Yardley. — 1st ed.
      p.cm.
    ISBN 978-0-06-137608-5
1. Coma—Patients—Fiction. 2. Upper class—New York (State)—Hamptons—
Fiction. 3. Neurologists—Fiction. I. Title.
    PS3625.A735R38   2008
    813'.6—dc22   2008006897

ISBN 978-0-06-226450-3

13 14 15 16 17   OV/RRD   10 9 8 7 6 5 4 3 2 1

Prologue

"This is fantastic," Rory Jacquard heard Oliver say from the balcony. "How did you find out about this place?"

"My father had pictures of it. I think he used to vacation here as a boy," she said, joining him. The sun was going down, bleeding crimson and orange into the impossible blue of the Caribbean. "Beautiful, isn't it?" she murmured, her heart pounding in her chest.

"Unbelievable," he said, then turned to her, smiling gently even as his eyes lit with hunger. "I'm glad you're sharing it with me."

She suddenly ignored the sunset, focusing on his intense stare and the gentle brush of his fingertips against her waist.

That's not all I'm sharing with you.

"Did you want to go down to dinner?" He nuzzled her neck, and she felt the tingle all the way down to the pit of her stomach.

"I'm not that hungry," she answered, her voice catching a little as he nipped at her jaw.

"Neither am I," he whispered against her ear. "Not for food, anyway."

Her breathing doubled in speed. It was going to be soon now. Any minute.

He turned her, stroking the sides of her sundress, breezing gently over the sides of her breasts while pulling her closer to him. She kissed him, bumping him a little too hard . . . clumsy in her eagerness. He laughed, even as she felt her cheeks burn.

"Sorry," she muttered.

"Don't be. I'm not." He kissed her back, more gently, a promise of things to come. Encouraged, she slowed down, reveling in the sensation of his lips and tongue. He cupped her breasts, his thumbs caressing the nipples beneath the thin material of her dress in slow, lazy circles, and she arched her back, pressing herself against his palms. "You are amazing," he said, against her mouth.

She smiled against his lips. He made her feel amazing. That was why she'd chosen him.

He held her against his rock-hard expanse of chest, and she nipped a quick kiss at his neck, then laughed. "You're salty."

"It's from Jet Skiing this morning," he said apologetically. "Why don't I take a quick shower, before we . . ."

He let the sentence trail off suggestively. If possible, her heart rate tripled. She nodded, unable to speak.

"I'll meet you there," he said, his eyes glowing as he nodded toward the bed. His smile was lazy, inviting, and she bit her lip against the wave of desire that pulsed over her like a tsunami. She watched as he retreated into the bedroom. Once he shut the door, she let out an explosive exhalation, then did a quick twirl, her skirt billowing out like a cloud around her body. She was so hot, she was surprised she didn't burn her clothes off her body, and it had nothing to do with the sticky, sweltering heat of the island.

She was going to have sex, for the first time in her life. Her body was so ripe for it, she felt ready to explode.

She hastily headed over to her suitcase, pulling out the dusty rose silk lingerie she'd purchased for just this occasion. She'd told her friends the trip was a graduation gift and birthday gift combined, treating herself to a trip to the Caribbean with her four-month boyfriend, Oliver. But she knew the real reason she was there, and she hadn't revealed it because she felt sure she'd be labeled a freak.

She probably wasn't the only twenty-one-year-old virgin on the face of the earth, but talking with her friends from college, listening to them gush about their boyfriends' skills in bed, or even complain about their lack of skills, made Rory feel like she was the only sexually inexperienced woman on the planet.

She tugged off the sundress and her underwear, then slipped on the teddy, loving the feel of the silk slipping against her bare skin. She'd showered as soon as they got back from the beach, anticipating this moment as she put on perfume strategically between her breasts, behind her earlobes. After a quick check in her makeup mirror, she climbed onto the bed, roughly combing her fingers through her hair. She hoped that it made her look sexy and rumpled.

She wanted tonight to be perfect.

She didn't think sex would hurt. After all, just because

she'd never had sex didn't mean she was completely igno-
rant. Besides her friends' play-by-play conversations, she
knew what an orgasm was—she'd felt it in the privacy of her
own bed, late at night, by her own hand. Nevertheless, all
the conversations and "practice" and substitutes in the world
weren't going to be the same as actually being skin on skin
with a living, breathing man.

The shower shut off, and after a few moments, Oliver
emerged. He didn't even bother with a robe. He strutted out
naked, his body solid, almost as beefy as a football player.
His hair was toweled dry, looking slick and dark auburn,
matching his pubic hair. Rory couldn't help it: she stared at
his body as if trying to memorize it. He was already hard,
and his penis bounced jauntily, the action matching his confident grin as he walked toward the bed.

She didn't mean to. She giggled. She'd never seen a penis
in the flesh before, as it were, and she had no idea it would
look so cheerful.

He frowned, pausing as he pulled back the sheet. "Something funny?"

She shook her head, hoping she hadn't offended him.
"This is a first for a lot of things," she said, by way of explanation. Oliver was the only person she'd ever admitted her
virginity to. He nodded, looking older than his own twenty-
two years. "Can I. . ."

She paused, her voice catching in her throat.

"Go on, can you what?" he asked, sliding into bed beside
her.

"Can I touch it?"

Now he laughed, and she brightened. "Of course," he said, lying back, his penis standing at attention. "Go ahead."

She put her hand out tentatively, her fingertips brushing against the bulbous tip of his cock. She pulled her hand away as if burned.

He laughed again. "It doesn't have teeth, Rory," he said. "Go on. Really check it out."

She laughed with him, nervously. For some reason, she had felt something . . . like a shock of electricity, something that made her whole system go intensely hot, then a slow, steady cold. Her fingertips still felt numb from the contact.

Stop stressing, she chastised herself. Years of family pressure and warnings might be haunting her, but they would not ruin this for her. She had let them dictate far too many of her life decisions: attending an all-girls school all the way through college, never bringing a boyfriend home, always afraid of the consequences if she disobeyed her far-too-strict parents. She'd been a coward. She'd waited far too long.

She was tired of being the good daughter. She wanted this, now.

She circled his shaft with her palm, surprised at how velvety soft the skin was and how solid and hard it had become, feeling like heated stone in her hand. She slid her hand awkwardly along his shaft, wondering at her own clumsiness. "I'm sorry," she whispered. "I don't know what I'm doing."

"Maybe I should take over now," Oliver said, his eyes alight.

She nodded, feeling words abandon her. She must be more nervous than she realized.

He started kissing her again, his hand stroking over the smoothness of her silk teddy. She leaned back against the pillows, allowing him more access as he moved over her breasts, causing her nipples to pucker and pout. She was breathing hard, her heart beating against her ribcage like a trapped bird.

"You don't need this," he said, sliding the teddy off of her shoulders and then slipping it off her hips and down her legs.

She felt vulnerable and yet incredibly aroused as the warm, moist tropical breeze from the open window hit her bare skin. She could smell mimosa and jasmine, a hint of guava. She could smell him, soap-clean from the shower. It was as if all her senses were heightened, with a pleasure that was so overwhelming, it was close to pain. Her head began to spin with it, and she fell against the pillow, fighting to stay in control.

"Don't worry. Trust me," he murmured against her shoulder. Then he moved forward, taking one of her nipples into his mouth, suckling softly.

She whimpered as the unbelievable pleasure rippled through her. Heat suffused her system, and she wanted to reach for him, hold his head tight against her breast, but her body felt immobile, all her reactions slowed to the point of stillness. Her heart raced impossibly fast, causing blood to rush in her ears, drowning out the sounds of the wild parrots and the crash of waves in the background.

He moved to her other breast, and she gasped. He was taking charge now, moving intently. This was why she'd chosen him, after all. He'd been the most determined, the most eager . . . the most seductive. He'd waited for her with relentless energy. He'd been both passionate and reserved.

She wanted tonight to be perfect, and now she was apparently so scared and so inhibited that she wasn't letting herself enjoy it.

She forced herself to murmur "Oliver" and then, with unbelievable effort, parted her legs slightly. He took the cue. While his mouth continued to work its magic on her breasts, his hands roamed, stroking the sensitive skin on the underside of her breasts before smoothing down to the gentle flare of her hips. His breathing was faster, too, and she could feel the hot, velvet tip of his penis stroking her thigh. His movements got less calculated as he pulled away, panting raggedly, and slowly stroked a finger over the delicate skin of her inner thighs. She let out an almost inaudible moan when his fingers parted her curls and pressed into her, tickling past her clit and into the damp passage beyond. The pleasure of his penetration was indescribable, and her whole body felt as if it were clamped down, a pressure cooker waiting to be opened and relieved.

"Do you like this?" His voice was raspy but confident. "Tell me what you want, baby. Let me know what you like."

Her tongue was heavy in her mouth. She tried to say something, but it came out as a low grunt.

He took that as a sound of approval, and he redoubled his efforts, alternating between licking at her breasts and her stomach while his fingers continued their slow and rhythmic penetration, in and out.

She wanted to spread her legs even farther, grinding her hips against the maddening sensation of his fingers. She wanted to reach for him, taste him, touch him. Pull him to her. She wanted to feel his hard, long cock replacing his hand, nudging against her pussy as he pressed inside her, filling her. She wanted to have the full experience, feel the dizzying release as a man pumped himself inside her hungry, aching need.

She struggled, but her muscles were completely unresponsive. She tried to say something. Her mouth locked in silence.

This is wrong, she realized. *Something's wrong.*

The pounding of her heart now had nothing to do with Oliver's ministrations. She felt fear, cold as an ice bath, drench her body.

This wasn't stress, or fear of disappointing her family, or maidenly nerves. This wasn't anything normal. She tried to make a noise, get Oliver to realize that there was something amiss, but he was too intent on pursuing his prize to notice.

She felt the warmth of his mouth withdraw as he stroked her legs, but she could no longer see him as her eyes drifted closed on their own, too heavy to fight against. She could smell her own arousal, mixed with the scents of the tropics. She could still hear the lullaby of the sea and her own slowing breathing. She couldn't move. She couldn't speak.

"This is it, baby," he said triumphantly. "No turning back. Are you okay?"

Help me, she thought frantically. *Help me, help me, help me . . .*

A pause. "It's all right, Rory. We're in no rush. You want me to slow down? Stop for a minute? Just say the word."

Not even a moan escaped her lips. Not even a sigh.

Finally she felt his body tense, the bed bowing slightly as he sat up abruptly. "Rory? Are you okay?"

She felt him get off the bed. He shook her slightly. "Rory? You're scaring the hell out of me. Come on, Rory." Another shake, harder this time. "Rory!"

He called her name, with increasing desperation, for another five minutes.

Rory never answered.

Chapter One

Dr. Jacob White pulled up to the large house in the Hamptons, pulling his Lexus to a smooth halt in the curving driveway. There was a crisp snap to the air. Fall was coming, and this place would go from the heights of the summer bustle to the dormancy of winter weather. *Strange place to keep a patient,* he thought as he rang the doorbell. Still, he wasn't here for the nightlife. He was here to cure someone who couldn't be cured.

In short, he was here to do his job.

A maid, dressed in a simple gray uniform, opened the door.

"I'm Doctor White," he said. "Mrs. Jacquard is expecting me."

She acknowledged this with a silent nod, then gestured for him to enter the house. The interior was sumptuous: dark wood paneling, lots of moldings. Everything expensive, tasteful, understated. He walked down a long corridor to a sitting room, where Mrs. Jacquard sat on a suede divan. She stood with effort. Although he would guess she was only in her sixties, she moved like someone much older. Her Chanel suit demurely projected old money and high society.

Which would explain the exorbitant amount she was offering to pay him, he thought. Not that he particularly needed the money, but it showed she was serious.

"Doctor White," she said, offering her hand. He shook it carefully, since everything about her seemed fragile. He sat after she did. "I'm so glad you've agreed to help my daughter. We've come very close to losing hope."

"I can't promise anything," he said off-handedly, "but I'm looking forward to the challenge."

Mrs. Jacquard cleared her throat, her tone hesitant. "She's been treated by a lot of doctors over the past six years."

Jacob smiled. *She's never been treated by me,* he thought.

"I should hope my record for recovery would speak for itself," he replied instead. "In any case, I will certainly do all I can for your daughter."

She nodded, her movements birdlike, small and delicate. "I suppose that's all we can ask," she said softly. "So many of the best minds in your field—Richards, Bjornsen, Hataki— have declined to treat her, saying there was no possibility of recovery."

That caused Jacob to start. The names she'd rattled off so casually were the ultimate experts in neurology. The fact that they'd turned down her case as hopeless made him feel uneasy. He hadn't done as much research into this case as he normally did before taking on a case.

He felt he hadn't needed to.

She was known in medical circles as "Sleeping Beauty," practically an urban myth among the neurological community: a young woman in a mysterious coma for six years, with no clear causation and no response, after a multitude of treatments. Curing her would be like finding the Holy Grail. When Mrs. Jacquard called, he found himself tempted by the challenge.

Now, he had to see if he had what it took, to find the solution to a puzzle that had all his peers stumped.

He all but rubbed his hands together, eager to get started. "I'm going to need all her case files," he said.

"So you mentioned," she said. "I've had all of her files put in your room. I hope you don't mind that we've set up a room for you here?"

"Not at all." He wasn't planning on sleeping much, anyway. There was too much work to be done. "It will be much more convenient this way. I'll settle in after I get a look at my patient."

Her eyes narrowed, and he wrestled with a surge of impatience. "Doctor White . . . what, exactly, do you know about my daughter?"

He shrugged. "I know that she was on a vacation in the Caribbean, that she fell into a coma, and that there was no clear reason for what caused it."

"You've heard the rumors, then." Her cultured voice was tinged with bitterness.

"Yes." He shrugged again. There was no point in denying it.

"My daughter did not use drugs," she said sternly. "There

was no group orgy, no rough sex that caused head trauma, no use of hallucinogens. She's a good girl. She's always been a good girl." She cocked her head, her bright eyes studying him. "Do you believe that?"

"Absolutely."

She stared at him, as if gauging the honesty of his reaction. After long moments, she relaxed against the back of her divan. "You mean that?"

"Of course."

"How could you tell?" she asked with a small smile.

"Because if she'd done any of those things," he answered, "it would have shown up for other doctors, and you wouldn't need me."

Her face fell.

"Mrs. Jacquard, I'm not here to judge your daughter," he said. "I've heard tons of crazy rumors, certainly, but I will tell you this: I am one of the best. I will go over the case files, but I am willing to bet that the reason your daughter is still under is because something was missed . . . something simple but vital. If there's anything nefarious in her past that might have contributed to her state—and consequently, might help wake her up—then I'll find it and use it. If that's a problem, then perhaps we shouldn't continue."

He waited, his body completely relaxed.

Her brow furrowed. Then she nodded.

"They said you might be a tad brusque," she remarked.

"I'm sorry for that," he answered. "But I get the job done."

"I certainly hope so." She stood, with some effort. "Well then, let's show you your patient."

He followed her down yet another corridor. The whole house seemed to have a strange silence to it, thick enough to touch. It was claustrophobic. He ignored the sensation, focusing instead on his excitement. This was the case that would be the signature for his whole career, he thought, his heart accelerating slightly.

She opened a door, pausing to look at him expectantly.

"This is my daughter."

He stepped in and was momentarily jarred. There were many familiar elements: medical monitoring equipment beeping faintly, the antiseptic scent that permeated every hospital he'd ever worked in. But the room was a girl's room. There were posters on the walls, teen idols from a decade ago. The walls were a faded robin's-egg blue. There was a desk, a television, a twin bed, as well as a dresser with small figurines on it. For a second, he anticipated seeing a child lying before him.

Then he got a good look at his new patient.

"What the hell?"

He shot a quick look at her mother. She obviously was used to a similar reaction. "She is your patient. This is my Rory."

He turned back, staring at the woman lying in the bed. Long, golden-blond hair flowed in waves across the pillowcase. Her skin was porcelain perfect, pale as pearl, yet with a glow of rose beneath the smooth softness that reminded him of a Rembrandt he'd seen years ago, brilliant with the artifice of life. Her lips were a dusky raspberry, pouting and full. Her long eyelashes rested on her cheeks like fringe.

He was expecting to see what he always saw, in a case like

this: the emaciated body of a young woman turned spindling and wan by the ravages of six years of coma. But she wasn't gaunt. Far from it, despite the IV hooked into her arm. From what he could see, she had a good shape, trim but womanly beneath her thin blanket. Her breasts rose and fell gently, her breathing unlabored. She looked like she was merely sleeping.

"What is this?" he demanded, his voice coming out hoarse. "Some kind of hoax?"

"This is what they can't explain," Mrs. Jacquard answered sharply. "This is why fourteen doctors before you have quit, and why twenty others have turned my requests down. This is why I called you." She paused, and when he looked at her, she seemed to be bracing herself. "Will you still take her on as a patient, Doctor White?"

His eyes were drawn back inexorably to the woman lying there, so beautiful, so perfect. So trapped. His whole body ached for a brief, confusing moment.

You should say no. The others had turned this case down for a reason, his logical mind argued sternly. He was good, but he wasn't a magician. There was no explanation for something this bizarre.

He took a step closer to the body. He should leave, he thought.

He touched her wrist. The pulse was weak, but stronger than he'd imagined. Her skin felt buttery soft, supple and sleek beneath his fingertips. He felt a pulse of heat shooting up from his hand, and he released her, momentarily stunned.

You should go.

He closed his eyes.

"What did you call her, again?" he asked.

"Rory," Mrs. Jacquard said. "It's a nickname, for Aurora."

"Rory," he repeated, and stroked her arm unconsciously. There was something here. More than his case, more than his career. There was something fascinating. Hypnotic. Compelling.

He leaned down, whispering gently.

"Hello, Rory. I'm Doctor Jacob White." He paused. "I'm here to wake you up."

"You should get some sleep, Doctor White," Carrie the night nurse suggested.

Jacob rubbed at his bleary eyes with the heels of his palms, struggling to focus on his watch. Two a.m. He had been sitting at the desk in Rory's room for the past seven hours, plowing through perhaps a third of the case files he'd been provided with. He'd seen different theories, different treatments, and different protocols. And not a single incident of progress: no blips on the brain wave monitors, no movements or speech, nothing.

It was not encouraging.

"Doctor White?" Carrie repeated, tentatively.

"Yes, yes. You're probably right." He gave the case files one last, longing look, then stood, wincing as his muscles screamed in protest at being kept cramped at the child-sized desk for so long. "I'm not going to get anything else done tonight."

His gaze shifted to Rory's sleeping form, still lying placidly beneath her beige blanket. "Good night, Rory," he found himself murmuring, patting her hand. "Don't worry, I'll keep going tomorrow."

When he turned away, he saw Carrie staring at him with a melting smile. "That's so sweet," she said. "Most of the doctors she's had have been so clinical and detached . . ."

"Good night, Carrie," he cut her off brusquely, then strode to his guest room, embarrassment speeding his steps. He'd never been a touchy-feely type of doctor: that was his brother Aaron's area, the psychiatrist. In fact, Aaron had often joked that Jacob chose to treat comatose patients so he wouldn't need to develop a bedside manner.

So why was Jacob talking to Rory? Especially when he, of all people, knew she was so deep and unresponsive, her brain waves so placid, that there was no way she could hear him?

"You need rest," he muttered to himself, stripping out of his clothes and crawling into the bed. He was just overtired. He'd regain perspective in the morning.

He was asleep by the time his head hit the pillow

Where am I?

Jacob blinked. He was in a hotel suite—a luxurious one, from the looks of it. Beyond a set of French doors was a beautiful view. He stepped closer. Far below, white sand beaches were lapped by aquamarine waves, and palm trees swayed in the soft, warm breeze. The suite was very high up, he noticed, in a sort of tower. He turned away from the balcony, examining the suite itself. A door opened from the living room to a sumptuous bedroom.

There, in the bedroom, was Rory.

She was no longer in a hospital gown, but a high-cut teddy of dusky rose-colored silk. She was swathed in ecru satin sheets.

She was still asleep.

He approached her slowly, his heart pounding, just as it had the first time he'd seen her. And, he admitted, every time he'd seen her since. What was it about this young woman that made his chest clench and his throat constrict? How did someone he didn't know, someone who *couldn't speak,* affect him so profoundly?

"Rory," he whispered. He touched her arm tentatively.

She stirred, turning restlessly toward him.

She moved.

He froze, his heart stopping, then starting at twice the speed. He stroked a long strand of hair away from her face.

"Mmmmm."

Sound! She'd made a sound!

Exultant, he felt excitement bubble through him like champagne, threatening to explode. He wanted to shout, jump, do *something* outrageous to celebrate this momentous occasion. Sound! Movement! After six years . . . holy *shit,* this was progress!

He punched the air with a low "Yes!" of victory, then leaned down, smiling, and kissed her on the lips, a quick, happy, thoughtless gesture.

Then he froze again, aghast at what he'd just done.

What the hell *are you thinking? You're a doctor! She's your patient! Are you insane?*

Remorse flooded through him, and he took a step back, castigating himself.

Suddenly, her eyes opened, followed by a series of languorous, sleepy blinks. Her dove gray eyes focused on his face.

"Who are you?" Her voice was sleep-husky, hoarse, and surprised.

For a moment, he forgot his own name. "Jacob," he finally said, too shocked to introduce himself properly.

"Jacob," she repeated, her voice like a low purr. She sat up. "Jacob. I've never . . . seen you before, have I?"

"No," he admitted, trying not to stare. Besides the miracle of her sitting up, he couldn't help but notice that the teddy was low cut in the front, showcasing her generous breasts in the most tantalizing way. He forced himself to focus on her face instead. That didn't improve matters: he found himself getting lost in those silvery eyes. He finally looked away, out the window, struggling to regain his control.

"Jacob," she murmured, and he was lost. He was drawn inexorably toward her, sitting down next to her on the bed. She reached out, cupping the side of his face, turning it toward her. "Your voice," she said softly. "It's so familiar, somehow."

Her palm was warm, her touch featherlight. It shouldn't have been arousing, but his muscles tensed, his cock going erect, his breathing shallow.

"Did you kiss me, Jacob?"

He swallowed hard. "Yes."

"I was asleep."

"Yes." Shame flushed his face.

She leaned forward. "Would you do it again? Now that I'm awake?"

He shouldn't. He knew he . . .

You're dreaming.

He paused, then chuckled to himself, taking a quick glance at his surroundings. He'd never been to a tropical island in his life. Of course this wasn't real.

"Jacob?"

He looked back at Rory, whose eyes were low-lidded, her full lips curving in a smile of sensual invitation.

He smiled back hungrily. Then, without a word, he leaned in.

This kiss wasn't a casual peck. This was a slow, thorough, sensual exploration. His lips covered hers, massaging them with insistent pressure. He coaxed her lips apart, nipping at her pouting lower lip with his teeth until she gasped in surprise. Then he traced the delicate flesh of her inner lip with his tongue, tickling, teasing. Hesitantly, her tongue crept forward, brushing against his. He twined his tongue with hers, his arms shooting out to grab her shoulders and pull her body flush against him. She moaned softly, her fingers smoothing up his chest before linking behind his neck, clinging to him.

The kiss broke out of control. He tilted his head, his mouth devouring hers, even as she molded herself against him. Their tongues tangled and mated. He felt her nipples, hard as pebbles, through the thin silk. He cupped her breasts with his hands, his palms holding her as his thumbs gently circled her areolae, caressing them until she mewled with pleasure and he felt her press to fit herself even more tightly against his eager fingers.

She tore her mouth away from his, throwing her head back.

He leaned down, his tongue tracing the valley between her full breasts, then dipping into the hollow of her throat. Her hand threaded into the hair at the nape of his neck, holding his head tight against her flesh. He changed angle, suckling hard at the column of her throat. Her gasp was a surprised cry of arousal.

He was burning. His cock pulsed and strained at the restrictive layers of boxers and trousers; his shirt was like a wool blanket, smothering him. He needed to feel his naked flesh, sliding along hers; his hips sliding between her thighs; his cock thrusting into her—

He shuddered, moving a critical inch away, his subconscious warning him . . . his professional instincts making one last, desperate bid for control.

"Jacob," she moaned, and tugged at the hem of his shirt, pulling it up, maneuvering it over his head and off his body. She stared at his chest with feminine satisfaction, the angled pink tip of her tongue licking her lower lip in anticipation, making her full lips glisten.

"Oh my God," he groaned, feeling a jolt of pre-come moisten his boxers. "I want to taste every inch of you."

Her eyes gleamed. "I want you to," she purred. With that, she slipped the straps of her teddy off her shoulders, shimmying until the garment was completely removed.

He was torn between staring at the beauty of her revealed form and ripping off his clothes so he could plunge into her warm, willing nakedness. He shed his remaining boxers and pants, stretching out next to her. Her eyes shone with excitement, eagerness—and, he noticed, a little nervousness.

He fought to slow down. He focused on her breasts, taking one in his hand while he slowly teased the other with his tongue, paying lavish attention first to one nipple, then the other, until she was breathing in short, ragged pants.

"Jacob," she whimpered, and he felt her hips moving restlessly against his. The brush of damp curls between her legs was almost more than he could bear, and he shuddered. He reached down, kissing the planes of her stomach as his fingers worked their way between her thighs. She parted her legs easily, her hips rising to meet him. He separated the tangle of curls. She was soaking wet for him. She cried out softly as his fingers pushed past the outer folds of skin, pressing into her.

She was tight, so incredibly tight. It was a struggle for even his index finger to penetrate. The thought of that snug, hot, wet pussy squeezing around the length of his cock had his body trembling with need. But she was too tight. He would hurt her unless he helped her out a little.

He pushed another finger in, slowly, carefully. Then he spread them, stretching her. She whimpered again, this time in discomfort.

Even though his body clamored for release, he positioned himself between her thighs, his hands on either side of her pussy. He parted her legs until he could see the vibrant pink flesh of her, her clit a hard, triangular bump. He leaned down, giving her a long, loving taste.

She cried out with pleasure, her body shaking, her thighs clamping on either side of his head. "Jacob," she gasped. "You shouldn't . . . you don't need to . . . oh God, I can't believe how that feels . . ."

He didn't respond, too intent on pleasuring her. He sucked on her clit, twirling his tongue around it until he felt her hips lift to meet his every swirling motion. He pushed his fingers deeper inside her, opening her, readying her for the larger, harder girth of his cock. She moaned loudly, bucking against him. He could feel her muscles, like coiled springs, on the brink of release.

His mouth worked frantically, suckling, nibbling, as his fingers plunged rhythmically inside her.

"Jacob!"

He felt the waves of contracting muscles, rippling over his fingers in undulating waves as her response trickled over his lips. He almost came himself, an answer to her unbridled abandon. He waited until she was finished, her coiled muscles going pliant. Then he eased himself up, his cock poised at the brink of her wet, fully stretched entrance . . .

"Doctor White!"

With a surprised grunt, Jacob felt his shoulder being shaken. He turned over . . . and promptly fell out of bed, hitting the floor. "Goddammit!" he shouted, and then looked up.

Carrie, the night nurse, was staring at him with concern. "I'm sorry, Doctor White, but you gave instructions to wake you if there were any, *er,* changes."

He felt his cheeks heat. "Shit." He abruptly realized that he was not wearing clothes . . . and that he had a hard-on the size of Texas. He grabbed the comforter, starting to drape himself with it before the import of her words sank in.

There were changes.

"What happened?" Ignoring the comforter, he grabbed a robe off the hook and threw it on, one foot out the door. "What's wrong? What happened?"

Carrie was obviously trying not to stare at his cock, which still tented out the terrycloth. "Her brain waves are showing . . . well, you'll have to see for yourself."

He growled, hurtling down the hallway to Rory's room. Glancing at her prone body, his cock throbbed painfully at the memory of what he'd been about to do.

Don't think about that!

Instead, he hurried to the monitor, picking up the pile of paper that was feeding through the brain wave device. His eyes looked over the results, then reviewed them again in stunned disbelief.

Normally, the lines were practically flat—a testament to the complete lack of activity of her brain waves. No matter what other doctors had tried, nothing had jarred that stubbornly still line.

Now, there was movement. Peaks, valleys . . . nothing radical, but considering her past, it was nothing short of amazing.

Carrie was at his side. "I thought you'd want to see it immediately."

"You were right." He turned to her. "What was happening? Did you do anything? Notice anything? What was going on?"

She shook her head, looking a little intimidated by the sharp rapid-fire of his questions. "I was just looking in on her, and I thought I heard the pen scratching," she said, gesturing to the device. "It was moving. I didn't understand what was going on. And nothing was happening. I wasn't even listening to the radio. It was completely silent in here, no one else was around." She tilted her head, studying him curiously. "Have you started treatment?"

"I didn't change anything," he snapped, then winced when she took a step back. "I'm sorry. I'm just . . . I'm still reading the files. I haven't had time to develop a treatment plan, much less enact one."

"Well, something must have happened," Carrie said thoughtfully.

He nodded. It figured. The biggest case of his career was now showing one of the most phenomenal turnarounds in medical history—and he had no idea what had happened, or why, because he'd been asleep. Worse, he'd been having one of the most erotic dreams of his life—about *her*. His *patient*.

And he didn't even get to have sex with her in the dream, to make matters worse. His cock still ached with unfulfilled need.

He gritted his teeth. He'd fallen asleep at his post. He was dreaming while something monumental occurred, just feet away. That wasn't going to happen again. From now on, he was eating, breathing, and *dreaming* about a way to cure this woman—and the next time she showed progress, he sure as hell wasn't going to be fucking some illusion while his career progressed without him.

Chapter Two

One week later, Jacob was at the end of his rope, and ready to hang himself from it.

"Every fucking one of the case files . . . ," he muttered, dropping a pile of manila folders on the floor in the guest room. "Been up with Rory, watching her every night. Getting practically no sleep at all. And I've still got *no* idea what caused the aberration."

He wanted to punch something. He wanted to break something. Even working out at the local gym had not gotten rid of his boiling frustration.

What had caused her brain to suddenly, finally react?

And why couldn't he re-create it?

He growled, deep in his throat, tossing his pen and sending it skittering across the desk.

He had no idea what had happened, and he had no clue how to proceed.

There was a knock on his door. "Yes," he barked.

It opened. It was Mrs. Jacquard, looking pale, as insubstantial as a ghost. "Doctor White?"

He sat up. "Yes, sorry. Is something wrong?"

He noticed abruptly that she was wearing a flannel nightgown, and her hair looked tousled. She was not her usual pulled-together, utterly presentable self. "I sleep at the end of the hall," she said, and her voice had shades of apology. "I thought I heard . . . noises."

He winced, his eyes looking at the stack of papers he'd dropped. His frustration was no excuse for the lack of professionalism. "I'm so sorry," he said, aghast. "I didn't mean to wake you."

"I know how hard you've been working," she said, her expression conciliatory. "You haven't slept more than an hour or two for the past few days."

Try eight days, he thought, suddenly feeling weary. Eight days, with nothing to show for them.

"I admire your tenacity. But perhaps you might consider resting." She paused. "Quietly."

He looked down, feeling chastened, embarrassed, and even angrier that he would act so completely out of character. He'd hit roadblocks before. Why was this making him so crazy?

"I can assure you, I won't be disruptive again."

"I mean it," she said, and her voice was gentle. "Get some rest." With that, she shut the door behind him.

He rubbed at his sandy eyes, then glanced at the bed.

Is work the only reason you've stayed awake?

Slowly, he stripped out of his clothes, climbing into bed almost tentatively. Which was stupid, really. So he'd had a sexy dream about a patient. Technically, sure, it was inappropriate . . . but it was his subconscious. He hardly had control over that. And at this point, he was hitting the wall, getting diminishing returns on all his hard work and missed rest. If he got some sleep, he'd be refreshed. He'd probably catch whatever it was he was missing.

He shut off the light, then lay back, feeling tension coiling through his body like a wary rattlesnake. He closed his eyes, breathing deeply.

As he started to fall asleep, he felt a chill of apprehension.

What is it about this woman?

But before he could formulate an answer, he had fallen into blackness.

He found himself back in the resort, back in the tower room . . . Rory's room. From a glance out the French doors, he could see a full moon lighting up the night sky. It had to be around midnight. When he'd been with Rory before, it had been daylight, late morning. Otherwise, nothing had changed.

Rory was back in her bed, sleeping. Her sheets looked tousled, tangled, as if she'd been tossing restlessly. She clutched at her pillow, her face frowning slightly.

His body went hard in a rush.

He'd been so powerfully close to completion before, when the nurse had interrupted him. And now, here she was, lying there like a Christmas present. She was naked beneath the light silk sheet. The full moon made her skin glow like mother of pearl. Her hair draped over the pillow in waves.

He was, he discovered, already naked.

All the better.

He moved the sheet aside, his eyes devouring the lines of her form: the lithe, graceful sweep from her shoulder to her hip; the long, almost artistic curve of her leg down to her delicate feet. Still sleeping, she turned onto her back, her breasts jutting upward, her nipples already rosy and puckered, eager for him.

He didn't wait, didn't think. He simply took and feasted.

He stretched out next to her, his cock already throbbing, and he trembled as the hot flesh of his cock head stroked inadvertently against the creamy smoothness of her thigh. He leaned down, kissing her hungrily as his hand moved upward to cup the fullness of her breast.

She gasped against his mouth, her hands going flush against his naked chest. Her eyes flew open, wide. He pulled back. "Rory," he growled, nipping at her jawline. "Rory. . ."

"Jacob . . ." She breathed his name with more longing and desire than he could ever remember hearing from anyone. Her hands no longer braced against his chest. They smoothed up the surface, holding his face, returning to the kiss with equal ardor.

His tongue swept inside, mating and tangling with hers as his hands cupped and cradled her breasts, his thumbs circling her nipples until they were as hard as his cock. She murmured against his mouth, incoherent, breathy sounds of passion. Her hips moved rhythmically, searching for connection. He nibbled at her full lower lip, and she made a mewling sound of pleasure as her fingers twined into the hair at the nape of his neck.

He was losing control. His hand shot down between them, his fingers pressing insistently between the curls at the junction of her thighs. They were already damp; he could feel the slickness of her response between the folds of her. She wasn't quite ready enough, he realized on some level.

"Jacob," she muttered. "I want to feel you . . . inside me . . ."

He shuddered. Then his fingers moved quickly, finding her erect clit and pressing with gentle firmness.

She cried out, her legs clamping down on his hand. Her hips bucked against his palm. Her curls were quickly soaked with the sweet juice of her pleasure, and he licked at her breasts as his hand continued to work feverishly between her legs.

Her nails clawed at his back, increasing his own passion. Her breathing was in short, choppy exhalations, her body shivering with each insistent thrust of his fingers. "I want you, Jacob," she moaned. "Please. Please."

He couldn't hold back. His own body was too hard, and he'd wanted her for too long. He nudged her until she was flat on the bed. She parted her legs, welcoming him, her eyes burning with passion. He covered her with his body, already moistened with sweat from the exertion of his control. He positioned his cock at the damp entrance of her pussy.

She was so incredibly tight. He could feel the taut flesh, embracing his cock head, giving him resistance as he pressed slowly inside her. She gasped, more of a surprised sound than one of pleasure, and with superhuman effort, he paused.

"Am I hurting you?" he asked, his voice hoarse.

"No," she murmured. Her eyes glowed, and she cupped his face. "I don't think you could ever hurt me."

He shuddered again. The trust in her expression almost made him come. He closed his eyes, unsure of how to accept such naked affection, even though his chest heated with something that had nothing to do with the act they were performing.

Blindly, he pressed in the rest of the way, feeling the rippling, rubbing muscles of her vagina massaging his cock like waves of molten passion. He groaned loudly. She felt so incredibly good, so hot, so *tight*, it was all he could do not to thrust harder, faster, feeling the snug passage caress and clamp against him until he found release.

He opened his eyes. Her expression still held tenderness, but now it held something else.

Wonder.

His chest expanded, and he withdrew slowly, a fraction of an inch at a time. Then he slid back inside her.

She gasped again, her head tilting back, and he could feel her hips lifting ever so slightly to meet his thrust. She swiveled experimentally. The feeling was outrageously pleasurable.

They continued like that: slow deep thrusts, then the maddening withdrawal. He'd never been with a woman like this, and the sensation of it, the extreme focus of the clenching muscles of her pussy against his cock was almost more than he could take. Her breathing was fast and labored, like his.

Her hips moved like a Balinese dancer's, smooth and sinuous, circling his cock, rubbing it with the suckling pressure
of her pussy.

"Oh God, Rory," he groaned, and started to pick up the
pace, his thrusts becoming more urgent.

"Yes," she answered, her voice a rough purr. "Please, yes. I
want to feel your cock all the way inside of me."

He wasn't expecting the direct command, and the surprise
of it sent a delighted shock through his system. He thrust hard
inside her, and she moaned, her hips lifting off the bed to match
him until he was fully buried inside her. She clawed at his back,
her legs twisting around his, trying as best she could to hold
her body flush against him, trying to get him even deeper.

He bucked against her, his thrusts moving, frenzied and
wild. She bit his shoulder as he sucked on her neck, their
pelvises moving quick and hard against each other, his cock
stroking inside her.

"Jacob," she said, and from the tension in her voice, he
could tell what was happening. "Jacob!"

He felt the contractions of her orgasm, rippling around his
cock, squeezing it mercilessly, milking his own orgasm out of
it. He cried out, his hips slamming against her as he emptied
himself inside her.

When it was over, he twisted, pulling her astride him,
keeping his cock buried inside her.

"You," she murmured, kissing him slowly. "I've been
waiting for you."

He kissed her back, feeling completely empty, vulnerable . . . and for the first time, tender.

"I've been waiting for you, too," he said, surprising her. Surprising himself.

"Rory, I—"

Before he could continue, he felt a sudden sharp jerking sensation. For a second, his senses blurred.

He was in bed—a different bed. A different woman was in front of him. It took him a few long moments to understand.

"Doctor White!" Carrie, the night nurse, was shaking him by the shoulders. He stared at her dumbly. "Doctor White, would you wake up?"

He blinked, then slowly slurred, "What? Who—what's happening?"

"It's Rory again," she said, her expression frantic. "Her brain waves . . . you told me to wake you if it happened again. It's happening now."

He nodded, then stumbled after her, only latching onto the thought that he must see Rory, must ensure that Rory was all right. He entered her room.

Carrie paused, her expression irritated. "Damn it! Now she's not."

"Now she's not what?"

Carrie sent him an odd look. "Doctor White, did you take a sedative? You seem groggy."

He shrugged, shaking his head. "No. Just hadn't slept in a while," he offered, mentally chastising himself to get it together. "I was too deep under. So, her brain waves reacted again?"

She nodded. "I was afraid I wasn't going to get to you in time."

He glanced at the paper feeding out of the monitor, look-ing at the wildly waving line. Out of his peripheral vision, he saw Rory's face. Her cheeks were lightly flushed, although otherwise she was the picture of serenity.

God, she's beautiful.

He caught himself and forced his eyes back to the paper as if they would be put out for daring to stare at her. "Again, what were the conditions?"

"Still nothing," Carrie confirmed. "No music, no speech. Only at night."

"Same time?"

"No," she said. "Last time it was one in the morning, this time it was three."

"What keeps causing this?" Jacob asked, rubbing his hand over his face. He didn't expect Carrie to answer, and she didn't. "Of course, she waits for the one night that I go to sleep to start acting up . . ."

"I'm sure you'll see it next time," Carrie said consolingly.

"Yeah," Jacob agreed bitterly. He'd damn well better.

"I'm going to go write this all down in the log," Carrie said, stretching. Then she left the room.

Jacob lingered, hovering over Rory's prone form.

Why do I dream about you?

His hand reached out, a bare inch over the curve of her cheek. He could feel the heat of her skin, reaching up to him . . . tantalizing him.

He pulled away.

"What is doing this to you?" he asked her softly.

And why do you affect me this way?

He closed his eyes. He wanted all his patients to recover, obviously. His success rate said as much.

But between the dreams, and the maniacal drive to find something, anything, to cure her, this was going above and beyond even his normal compulsive behavior.

He opened his eyes to find her still lying there, motionless, pristine . . . perfect.

"I'll stay awake next time," he promised, adding silently, *I can't keep dreaming of you. Not that way. Not if it makes me feel like this when I'm next to you.*

He stepped away carefully. "I'll see you in the morning, Rory," he said, venturing back to bed. He wondered if he'd be able to keep his promises . . . especially when a part of him knew he really didn't want to. He wanted to wake her—but he also wanted, no, *needed*, to touch her again.

And dreams were the only way that was possible.

He recognized the room immediately: the sumptuous suite, the phenomenal view, the palatial balcony. He was in the tower room of the island resort, again.

He was naked, he noticed in passing. Just as he had been, when last he was in this room.

He glanced over toward the bedroom. The door was ajar.

Rory was not in the bed.

He heard a sound—water rushing—that owed nothing to the crashing waves below. He moved forward, almost hesitantly, moving past the bed until he reached the door of the bathroom.

Rory. In the tub.

Holy hell.

She leaned back against the lip of the tub, that glorious blond hair spilling over the edge of the marble like a waterfall of molten gold. Her face was drawn with passion, her eyes closed, head tilted back. Her breasts were tight, her rose-colored nipples taut and erect with passion. Her legs were splayed, her feet resting on the rim of the tub. She held the showerhead between her legs, directing the water at the spread lips of her pussy, like a vibrant pink flower. She gasped in pleasure as the water drenched her sex, her hips writhing beneath the demanding spray.

His whole body tensed. His cock sprang to life in a rush, watching the unbridled, unashamed display before him.

She was murmuring, sensual gasps and incoherent words of pleasure. When she cried out in orgasm, he could feel the dampening of pre-come on the tip of his penis, and his body jolted involuntarily.

This is a dream, some quiet, cold part of his mind pointed out. *It's just a dream.*

There were no restrictions here. No rules. Nothing but desire.

She rested the nozzle back in its holder, and her gray eyes slowly fluttered open, slowly focusing on him. He stared at her hungrily.

"Jacob?" she asked, her voice husky and low. She looked at him through the fringe of her lashes, and a pretty blush rode high on her cheeks. "I thought you were . . . I don't know. A hallucination or a dream or something."

He nodded.

You didn't want to dream about her again.

Apparently his subconscious had other ideas.

She stood up, climbing gracefully out of the tub. Her body was spectacular: long limbed and lithe, the sinuous, womanly curves of her as delicate and precise as if they'd been painted by Michelangelo. She glanced at him nervously.

"I guess this must be a dream," she said, then she smirked at him, her cheeks pitting with two mischievous dimples. "Because in no other place in my life would a gorgeous naked man catch me doing *that* in the bathtub. I don't suppose you . . . how much did you see?"

"Everything," he said, watching as her blush deepened a few shades.

"I'm sorry."

"I'm not." His body tensed. "I'm glad."

"You weren't embarrassed?" she asked.

"It turned me on."

She looked down, seeing his rock-hard cock standing at attention. Her blush deepened, but she didn't look away. He noticed that her nipples tightened a little.

"What if this is a dream, Rory?" he murmured. "A strange man catches you naked in the bath and says he wants to make love to you. Would you let him?" He reached out, boldly stroking her breast, watching as she gasped, her pupils dilating. "Will you let *me*, Rory?"

He saw her pulse, beating hard in the column of her throat. She took a step forward.

"Yes," she whispered.

He held his breath. He no more could have stopped himself from touching her than he could have stopped the tide from coming in.

He leaned down, and she tilted her head up, meeting his lips. The kiss started soft, a light brush of his lips against hers . . . coaxing, teasing. She made a low sound, like a delighted purr, and he found himself smiling against her mouth. She nipped at his jawline, obviously impatient. He slicked his tongue over her full lower lip. When she gasped, he took advantage, sweeping his tongue between her parted lips, caressing her tongue with his own in a long, deep kiss.

"More," she breathed. She pressed against him, her damp skin sliding along his. He groaned, his mouth moving over hers more intently as his hands shot out to grip her hips, holding her flush against him, trying to stop the delicious friction she was building.

She gripped his shoulders, outmaneuvering him by dragging her breasts against his chest and gasping against his mouth as she struggled to bring her pelvis in closer contact with his. His cock nestled against her stomach, and he shuddered at the feel of her soft, warm skin pressing against him in even such a tangential way.

"You put your mouth on my pussy," she murmured, and the words caused him to groan in anticipation. "You made me come."

"Yes," he said, in a strained voice.

"Then, the next time," she whispered, "you put your cock inside me, pleasuring me with your hardness, until I came."

"Yes," he said. "Oh God, yes."

"Ever since I met you, I haven't been able to eat, I haven't been able to sleep," she said quickly. "My body is fevered, *all the time.* All I can think about is you: the way you taste, the way you touch me, the feel of your tongue, and the feel of your cock as you push inside me . . ."

"God." The words lashed against him, making going slow almost impossible. "I'm going to take you on the floor if you keep talking like that."

"Take me wherever," she said, her hands rubbing against his restlessly. "Just take me."

"No," he said firmly. "Trust me, there's more to this than being quick."

He carried her, still wet from her bath, over to the bed, dropping her on its surface. She laughed softly when she tumbled onto the coverlet. She was reaching for him before he could stretch out beside her. "Jacob," she repeated, before her mouth covered his chest in a flurry of kisses.

"I don't want to rush," he explained with a wry smile. "I want to take my time, draw it out . . . show you how we can both enjoy this. But damn it, woman, you're making it hard not to. I can't remember wanting anyone this badly."

He wrapped his arms around her, submerging himself in the feel of her. He stroked his palms along her shoulders, down her arms, lacing his fingers in hers as he nuzzled kisses in the hollow behind her ear, then along her jaw and throat. She laughed again, breathy and aroused and joyful . . . and then she wrapped her legs around his, twining around him like vines. His heard thudded heavily in his chest. Each gasping breath he took was infused with her wonderful scent, equal parts flowers, spice, and sheer femininity. He felt his control start to snap. He lapped at her breasts, tasting the water from her bath as well as her skin. Her hands grasped his hard-on when he took one firm nipple in his mouth, sucking intently, letting his teeth graze against the pebbled point.

"Yes," she said, shifting against him, her leg sliding along his until her knee anchored on his hip.

He could feel his cock stroking along her thigh, felt the bulbous tip brush against the damp curls of her pussy. He gritted his teeth as his hips moved toward her, involuntarily, like metal to lodestone.

"Please, Jacob," she begged. "I want to feel your cock inside me . . ." She freed her hands from his, wrapping her arms around his torso. "I want to feel you pushing inside me, filling me."

"Rory . . ."

"We can go slow later," she promised. "But I can't wait . . ."

"Rory," he groaned, and the dam of his self-restraint broke. He pressed her onto her back with his knee, then angled himself between her thighs. With a free hand, he reached down between them to guide his cock into her wet, snug entrance. Poised there, he paused, looking deeply into her eyes.

Slowly, he moved his hips, penetrating her by inches, ignoring the primal urge to bury himself in her quickly. She moaned, her hips arching to meet him, her legs wrapping around his as his cock delved deeper into her pussy. He could feel the warm walls of her cunt contracting around him; every swirl of movement from her hips caressed his cock in a maelstrom of sensation, and he groaned, withdrawing slightly.

She whimpered. "Deeper," she encouraged, her fingernails digging into his back in a way that drove him wild. He pressed in deeper, then withdrew, repeating and continuing until his entire shaft was buried inside her, his cock head brushing against the back wall of her cunt. He alternated his movements, circling inside her as he continued his sexual onslaught. She murmured his name, over and over, and her cunt tightened around him like a moist fist, stroking him, milking his member until he was shaking and couldn't see straight.

"Rory," he pleaded, his hips moving faster of their own accord.

"Yes," she breathed, her eyes closed, white teeth biting that delicious full lower lip. "Just like, oh, *that*, right there . . ."

His movements turned frantic, his hips bucking against her. He leaned down, hooking his hands beneath her knees, bringing her to a more extreme angle, plunging even deeper inside her. She cried out, and he stopped for a fraction of a second, afraid he'd hurt her.

"Yes!" she screamed, her hips rocking against his cock in a mindless frenzy of desire.

He snapped. He pounded inside her, pulling her to him. When she let out a rippling cry of orgasm, he felt every convulsive spasm around his cock, and he was punched with an orgasm of his own. He collapsed against her, his cock spurting inside her as his hips rocked and jolted with the almost painful intensity of his release.

"Damn it," he said, when his sanity returned. "How do you do that?"

"How do I do what?" she said, her voice sleepy-happy.

"Make me lose control."

"Just lucky, I guess," she said, with a delighted laugh. "Why? Want to teach me another lesson?"

He shouldn't have been able to. His body should have been wrung out. But, to his surprise and gratitude, his flagging cock was already gearing up for a second round. "You ready for another lesson?"

She sat up, smiling. "Yes." Her eyes shone like diamonds.

"Well, we're a little messy right now," he said thoughtfully. "Do you mind taking another bath?"

"A bath." Her mouth tested the word, rolling it around thoughtfully. "Okay."

He filled the tub with fragrant bubbles, knowing she was feminine enough to appreciate it. The water was just this side of hot. He sank in, then beckoned to her to join him. It was a large, deep marble bath, comfortable enough for the two of them.

He lifted her until she was lying on top of him. When she went to straddle him, he nudged her legs closer together, until they were almost closed. Then he slipped his penis in between her soap-slicked thighs, slipping up and past her clit into her still-soaked pussy.

She gasped, clinging to him.

"See?" he said, his voice strained. He slid her up his body, withdrawing, then nudged her back down, burying himself fully within her again. "Now . . . what do you think of slow?"

"I like it," she said breathily, moaning with pleasure as he entered and retreated, pressing up and inside her, then withdrawing enough to drag his cock down her sensitive thighs. The friction of her body sliding along his was enough to make his cock rock hard, but he prided himself on his control. Her breasts dangled invitingly in front of his mouth in this position, so he indulged himself, sucking first on one, then the other, running his tongue along her rosy tipped nipples, circling the areola. She gasped, pressing her breasts more firmly into his mouth as her hips tilted back, increasing his penetration.

Suddenly, there was a knocking sound. Rory didn't seem to notice: her breathing had gone shallow, and she was beginning to move her hips, sliding up and down his body, taking him deeper and deeper inside her.

Then he felt like someone was shaking him.

No, not yet, not yet . . .

He started thrusting inside Rory with more insistence, more intensity. She wrapped her legs around his hips, impaling herself on his cock, riding him like a horse. He groaned, rolling his head along the tub's edge as the feel of her pussy mounting his cock milked him like a fist. He groaned, thrusting upward as she plunged downward, feeling her clamp around him. "Rory . . ."

She cried out, and he felt the echoing reverberations of her orgasm rippling over the sensitive flesh of his cock. He groaned, his body jerking as he came like a gunshot, the sensation blasting through him like lightning.

"Doctor White!"

He closed his eyes, then opened them.

He'd locked his door. Carrie was pounding on it impatiently.

"Just a minute," he muttered. He'd ejaculated in the bed. He would need to clean up. He grimaced, wiping himself off, throwing on a robe. "What?" he barked out.

"You missed it *again*," she said sharply. "Are you sure you're not taking a sedative? I've been knocking on that door for five minutes!"

He closed his eyes. "No, I'm not taking a sedative," he growled. "I'm just . . . a deep sleeper, is all."

"Well, you told me to warn you when Rory's brain patterns changed," she returned. "If you don't want me to do that—"

"No, you did the right thing." He went to Rory's room, where he studied the printout.

Her skin, he noticed, looked rosy. Was it a trick of the light?

He got a little closer, studying the complexion of her face. *Just as perfect as in his dreams,* he thought. He took a deep breath. There, under the antiseptic smell of the room, was the scent of *her* . . . delicate, reminiscent of some exotic flower, like hibiscus or jasmine or—

He jerked back abruptly.

This was his patient.

As long as his feelings were contained to the realm of dreams, he thought, backing away from Rory, *well, that would be one thing.* But his dreams were starting to affect his real life.

He was going to have to be very, very careful.

Another two weeks had passed, and Jacob was sitting at Rory's desk, staring at her sleeping form, his hand scribbling notes that would make no sense to him when he reread them later. Thankfully, his handwriting was, like most doctors', inscrutable.

"Do you have an appointment, Doctor White?"

"*Hmmm?*" Jacob glanced over at nurse Carrie, barely realizing she'd been in Rory's room with him. "No. Why?"

"You've been looking at your watch every five minutes," she pointed out, adding, "for the past two hours."

"Have I?" He cleared his throat. "I wasn't aware." Then he stretched and said with elaborate casualness, "I'm tired. I guess I'll turn in."

"Going to sleep already?" Carrie asked, her eyes widening. "It's only eight."

"Eight?" He shifted uncomfortably. "Well, there isn't anything else I can do in here. I'll just go to my room and . . . go over some, ah, research."

"All right, Doctor."

He didn't know why he felt defensive, but he tacked on an additional excuse. "It's been getting dark so early, I feel like it's midnight."

She was wearing a dubious expression, and so he realized it would be of no use to elaborate further. He cleared his throat again, switching subjects hastily. "I've set up a video camera, so there's no reason to wake me if there's any change in her condition. I'll just watch the tapes the following day."

"That's probably a good idea," Carrie agreed. "It seems like every time I wake you up, you never get here in time, anyway. It's like she *waits* for you to fall asleep."

"It does seem so, doesn't it?" he said, and laughed nervously. "Good night, Carrie."

"Good night, Doctor."

He nodded, hurrying out of the room. His palms were sweating. He hastily got to his own guest room and shut the door, locking it. Then, briefly, he leaned back against the hard wood of the door frame, closing his eyes.

He'd been fighting the urge to go back to bed since noon. Not because he was tired—although he was, desperately so. A night's worth of dreams often left him more exhausted than a day's worth of work. No, he wanted to get back to bed so he could get back there, to his dreams.

Back to her.

He'd dreamed about her every night for the past two weeks. If this kept up, he was going to have to call Aaron, he knew that. But for now, he thought that perhaps his subconscious was simply working overtime to provide him with a sort of background for his latest patient project. Normally, he never got to "know" his patient, except from apocryphal data, anecdotes from family members, and case files.

This was one of the biggest cases of his career. If he was creating a character study in his mind to get closer to her . . . well, where was the harm, right?

You're justifying, his conscience commented critically. *Like an addict.*

He ignored that, stripping quickly, dousing his light, and scrambling beneath the covers. He tossed and turned fretfully, excitement making his body tremble slightly. He felt ridiculous—and impatient.

Finally, when darkness enveloped him, he welcomed it.

* * *

"Rory." Her name was on his lips before his eyes were open, and he felt her body press against his.

She held him tightly, her head tucking under his chin. "Jacob." He could hear the smile in her voice before he saw it curving her lips. He kissed her happily. "You're back."

Back from where? The comment was odd, but it wasn't enough to distract him from the fact that he could feel her naked skin beneath his fingertips. "I couldn't wait to see you," he found himself saying, stroking a wayward lock of hair away from her face.

She was always so warm, so inviting. It felt as if her entire world revolved around him. He nuzzled at her neck, breathing in the floral, spicy scent of her.

"Jacob," she purred, and the mere sound of her voice was enough to have his muscles tensing in familiar excitement.

"Aren't you getting tired of me?" he teased, nipping at her earlobe.

"Not remotely," she answered fervently. Then she paused, and he could read the hesitation in the way her body stiffened. "Are you? Getting tired of me?"

He guided her hand down to his cock, smiling when she giggled. "Does that answer your question?"

She kissed him, hungry, her mouth hot and mobile against his. They stayed like that for long minutes, simply tasting each other, their hands exploring as their mouths savored the sensations of friction and wet heat, lips, and tongues.

He pulled away. "Sweetheart, you're going to kill me with sex."

He hadn't realized gray eyes could sparkle, but hers did, bright with mischief, when she said, "I wouldn't be so addicted to it if you weren't so good at it."

He leaned back in the bed. "I can't remember ever feeling like this before."

"Turned on?" she joked, giving his cock a light, playful squeeze.

He smiled back. "Happy."

The comment must have surprised her, because she let go of him, then put her arms around his shoulders, embracing him tightly but not seductively. "I'm glad," she whispered, and he felt an expanding feeling in his chest. "You make me happy, too."

For the next few minutes, they sat on the bed, holding each other, hugging each other tenderly. It was the closest he'd ever felt to anyone. He closed his eyes, clutching her tighter, as if he were afraid he'd lose her.

Finally, as if afraid of his own emotions, he cleared his throat. "You know, I think we need a little change."

"A change?" she echoed, when he disengaged, getting off the bed and standing up. "You mean . . . you don't want to . . ." She gestured at the rumpled sheets.

His grin was wolfish. "Oh, I 'want to,' all right," he said, reassuring her. "I just thought maybe we should leave this room."

"Leave?"

"There's more to the hotel, right?" He held out his hand to her, beckoning her. "And plenty of spots outdoors. Let's explore."

She clutched the sheet to her, her eyes wide. "*Ummm . . .* maybe we should stay inside."

"Why?"

"There are some parts of the island that aren't safe." Her gray eyes were troubled, storm-cloud dark. "Better avoided. I can take you to the beach, if you'd like, but otherwise . . ."

"All right." He hated seeing her so agitated. He took her hand, tugging her off the bed. "We'll stay inside, then. You must know this hotel like the back of your hand."

"Pretty well," she demurred. She started to open the closet, reaching for a dress.

"Why bother with clothes?" he asked curiously. "There's no one else here, right?"

"Not that I've seen," she said. "Not up in the hotel, no."

He wanted to pursue it, but she still put on a dress, pulling it over her head. It was slate blue, making her skin glow ethereally. She slipped on a pair of shoes, then looked at him expectantly. He quickly put on his own clothes, which were piled on the floor. He would feel stupid, walking naked next to her.

They walked out into the hotel, and he found himself holding her hand as they strolled down the empty hallways. He'd never held hands with anyone that he could recall. It felt natural.

"What would you like to see?" She led him to the large, ornate lobby. "Are you hungry? There's a fantastic kitchen in the restaurant. Or maybe you'd like to try the spa?"

He thought about it. The idea of taking her in a hot tub was intriguing . . . but, then, so was the idea of experimenting with some food. "Your choice," he said, squeezing her hand gently.

"Let's try the spa," she suggested, her mouth quirking in a tiny catlike smile. "I could use a little . . . relaxation."

She led him down to the basement level. The spa, like everything else in the resort, was luxurious, five-star all the way . . . and empty. They walked past the deserted reception desk to the spa itself, where he could hear the burble of hot tubs and see the redwood planking of a sauna room. "What would you recommend?"

"*Hmmm.*" She chuckled. "The regimen is sauna first, to loosen up. Then a quick dip in the pool, to tighten things up." She winked, and he found himself laughing. "Then maybe a massage, for full relaxation. How does that sound?"

"I put myself in your capable hands." He felt his blood warming, and better still, he felt a peculiar lightness of mood. It was like playing. When was the last time he'd played?

They stripped down again—"Told you we didn't need clothes" he groused, to which she answered with a light swat on his backside—then headed for the sauna, wrapped in towels. Opening the door was like opening a furnace. The heat was dry and yet almost oppressive. He closed the door behind them as she poured water over the heated rocks, causing steam to billow, filling the room. He sat down, expecting her to sit next to him. Instead, she sat slightly farther away, almost primly. "You're the one who wanted a change," she reminded him, tightening her towel around her. "So why don't we try talking?"

"Talking?" He said it with overemphasized schoolboy

petulance, and she laughed in response. "I didn't agree to *talking*."

"Tell me about yourself." Her voice was smooth, inviting. "Where are you from? What were you like as a child?"

He felt tension creep up his back at the question. "I grew up in New York," he said. "But I've traveled all over. And I guess I was like any other kid."

She was quiet for a moment, and the heat wrapped around them, filling in the spaces between their words. Finally, she nodded. "What made you so unhappy?"

"Unhappy? I didn't say I was unhappy."

She scooted closer. "You didn't have to."

He fell silent for a long moment, then took a deep breath of the scalding sauna air. "My parents were—are—very famous doctors. Cardiologists. Their work has always been very important to them. We traveled a lot because of that."

"We? Do you have family?"

"One little brother—Aaron. Sort of the black sheep of the family."

She shifted slightly. Perspiration started to trickle down her neck, and he watched it trace a slow, hypnotic line from her collarbone to the valley between her breasts. "What, Aaron isn't a doctor, like you?"

He let out a startled snort. "No, he's a doctor—but a psychiatrist. And that hardly counts." He laughed, shaking his head. "Sorry. I make fun of him about that constantly."

"So you're a doctor, too?"

"*Hmmm?*" The question caught him off guard. "Yeah. A neurologist."

"Neurologist," she repeated—and a strange expression crossed her face, as if she were trying to remember something.

I'm your doctor, he thought . . . and guilt, sharp and piercing, immediately assailed him. He cleared his throat. "What about you?" he asked. "What do you, ah, do?"

"Nothing." She smiled, but the action wasn't echoed in her expressive eyes. "I was a college student, just graduating."

"You 'were' one," he echoed. "What happened?"

"I came here."

A symbol, he thought. The island, in his subconscious, represented the coma. Interesting.

She snuggled up against him, and all thought of symbolism and the subconscious receded. "Are you hot enough yet?"

Sweat misted his body, crawling over his skin in small rivulets. She looked incredible, her hair curling in loose gold waves, her skin dewy. She smiled at him.

He stroked a palm over her slick skin, reaching for her towel. "I'm getting there," he rasped.

She danced away, leaving him with only the towel as she opened the door. "Time for the pool, then," she taunted, moving away from him.

He followed her, tossing the towels to one side. The pool was large, a glowing, iridescent blue. She dove in cleanly, emerging at the far end of the pool with a gasp. Her laugh was as clear and clean as the water. "Come on in," she invited, her voice husky.

He followed her lead, and then he froze, almost literally, when his body hit the water. He came up sputtering. "Cold!"

She laughed. "You said you—"

"—wanted a change," he completed, his body slowly acclimating to the temperature. "You know, if you want to turn a guy on, cold water isn't really going to help matters."

"Poor, poor baby," she cooed, mocking him. Then she swam next to him, as graceful as a mermaid, her body mere feet away from his. His body was caressed by the currents of water she created. When he reached for her, she remained just out of grasp, mischievous, tantalizing.

"You must have been cruel as a child," he teased as he stalked her across the pool.

Her breasts floated on the water. She glistened with beads of wetness on her skin and eyelashes. Instead of laughing, she looked thoughtful.

"I was tenderhearted when I was a little girl," she replied instead. "At least, that's what my parents tell me. I took in a stray when I was five years old."

"Lots of kids do." He worked on cornering her by the pool stairs.

"Yes, but this was a stray raccoon." She laughed. "I had no idea how dangerous it was. I called him Mackie, and I loved him dearly until my parents took him away."

He paused. "You must have been heartbroken."

She paused, too, no longer trying to evade him. "I was," she said. "But they explained to me that it was too dangerous to me. They were always telling me I had to be more careful. I don't know why, but they always seemed to think that bad things might happen to me." She smiled wanly. "They loved me very, very much. But it was a little stifling."

She sounded so melancholy. He held her to him, and she let him, snuggling against his chest. He kissed her shoulder, the crown of her head, stroking her back comfortingly.

Then he felt the heat of her body, warming him. His cock crept upward hopefully.

She smiled. "Ready for that massage now?"

He nodded.

They walked to the massage area. It was warm and dimly lit. "Why don't you stretch out," she said softly, "and I'll rub you down."

He did as instructed—lying on his back, his cock standing at full attention. She toweled him off, then squirted some massage oil in her hands. It smelled like almonds and vanilla. When she smoothed the warm lotion over his skin, he groaned softly. "That feels great," he encouraged.

With long, loving strokes, she massaged his arms, down the planes of his chest, circling his abdomen. She ignored his most prominent part, opting to rub his thighs and legs, even massaging his feet. Despite the ratcheting sexual tension building in his body, he was surprised to find himself melting beneath her ministrations. He'd never gotten a massage before. While he doubted that any massage would be as gratifying as one from a beautiful naked woman, he realized that maybe he should have taken time to enjoy the occasional—

"Now, the hard part," she interrupted his thoughts, her eyes gleaming. And with that, she leaned over his cock, placing her mouth on it.

He gasped in surprise, then in pure enjoyment as she suckled gently on the head. He could feel her tongue tracing the tiny fissure at the tip, then circling the mushroom cap edge. She took him in deeper, her tongue gliding down his shaft. He balled his hands in fists, his hips rising unconsciously to meet her hot, luscious mouth. She retreated, then took him in even deeper. Her movements were awkward, even a little clumsy, but the enthusiasm and her obvious enjoyment of the task more than made up for any missteps.

"Rory," he murmured, his fingers clutching at the sheet on the massage table. "God, Rory . . ."

She continued the rhythmic motion, sucking and withdrawing, taking him in deeply. With one hand, she cupped his balls, tickling their undersides, then scratching her nails lightly down his thighs. He was ready to explode, when she finally pulled away, gasping. "Was that . . . all right?" she asked, out of breath.

He didn't answer. Instead, he swung his legs over, lifting her up. She parted her legs willingly, and he positioned himself at her cunt, pulling her flush against him. He slid in easily—she was already dripping wet. That she was turned on by sucking on him was enough to push him right to the edge. She wrapped her legs around his waist, and he lifted and lowered her, his cock plunging inside her as she rocked against him. Her breasts crushed against his chest, and they kissed, their tongues matching the rhythmic in-out of their sex.

His orgasm blasted through him, and he cried out, shuddering against her. She gripped his back, her thighs clenching as she squeezed against him. She echoed his orgasmic shout, holding him tight, the two of them trembling.

He rolled onto his back, staying inside her, stretching her out on top of him. "You are amazing," he murmured. "If this is a dream, I don't think I ever want to wake up."

"It's not a dream," she murmured. "It's real. We're real."

We're real . . .

He held her tight. It didn't feel like a dream anymore.

Chapter Three

"Jesus, Aaron," Jacob grumbled. "Your apartment looks like a shrink's office."

"Can't help that. I'm a shrink," Aaron replied, handing Jacob a glass of scotch. "On the rocks, right?"

Jacob shrugged, taking a swig of the amber liquid. The quick hit of fire did nothing to calm his nerves, and his scowl deepened.

Aaron sat down in an armchair, gesturing to his couch. Jacob shook his head. "So, what brings my big brother all the way to Manhattan and away from his cushy gig in the Hamptons?"

Aaron's tone was playfully mocking, but his expression was curious and incisive. Jacob paced over the thick beige carpet, like a panther at a very chic, monochromatic zoo. "I'm having trouble with this case," he admitted.

"Of course it's work related," Aaron replied easily. "Neurology's not my field, but if you want to bounce some theories, I'd be happy to listen."

"That's part of the problem. I don't have any theories. I don't have anything."

"That's got to be frustrating." Aaron leaned forward in his chair.

"Don't pull the sympathetic psychiatrist counseling bullshit on me, okay?" Jacob finished his drink, put the glass down on the wet bar, then rubbed his hands over his face. "The thing is it's not the case itself. The problem's with me."

"You?"

"If you repeat this to Mom or Dad," Jacob said sharply, "I swear, I'll—"

Aaron interrupted this with a laugh. "Since when have our parents ever called us for casual conversations? Or been interested in our lives? Relax. Jesus, you're wound like a watch."

Jacob sighed, finally forcing himself to sit down. "I don't know what the hell's wrong with me," he muttered. "No, I do know what's wrong with me. It's this case. It's this woman."

"Woman?" Aaron's eyes widened. "Not anyone you're dating, obviously. Who, then? Your patient?"

"I've been dreaming about her," Jacob said slowly.

"Oh?" Aaron's face held no judgment. "How so?"

"Intense dreams." Jacob clenched his jaw, then reluctantly continued. "Sexual dreams."

"I see." Aaron was still noncommittal. "How often?"

Jacob closed his eyes. "Every night."

Aaron was silent.

Jacob opened his eyes, taking a deep breath. "For the past month."

"Every night for the past month," Aaron echoed. His face was impassive, but Jacob knew him well enough to read him: he was shocked and concerned. Jacob sank lower into the seat. "Same dream, every time?" Aaron asked.

"No." Jacob felt his body shiver at the mere thought of last night's dream. The feel of Rory, the perfumed scent of her body as his mouth worshiped her skin, her breasts . . . her pussy. "It's different. It's almost chronological, as if I enter a different world as soon as I go to sleep."

"That's unusual." Aaron had shifted into clinical mode, and for that Jacob was thankful. "But the dreams are always sexual. Do you have conversations?"

Jacob thought about his conversation with Rory, in the spa. He hadn't revealed that much to women he'd dated for several years. "We've talked," he finally admitted. "Still, the emphasis is usually on the sex."

"Interesting." Aaron tapped his fingers on the arm of his chair. Jacob knew Aaron was itching to take some notes, as if Jacob were one of his patients. Thankfully, Aaron seemed to be resisting the urge. "This case. Is it particularly important to you?"

Jacob nodded impatiently. "This case is my magnum opus," he said. "It's a long shot, but she's legendary. I wake her up, and my future's guaranteed."

"Your future's already guaranteed," Aaron pointed out. "So why this?"

"She's a challenge," Jacob said.

"Let me guess: a lot of your peers have tried to cure her and failed."

"So?" Jacob replied defensively.

"I know your ego, big brother," Aaron said. "She's your quixotic dream patient. You want to cure the incurable. You want the glory."

"I suppose." But even as Jacob said it, something wasn't ringing true about the statement. It had been true, especially when he first met Mrs. Jacquard and initially took on the job.

Something had changed since then.

"You want the acknowledgment," Aaron pressed. "You've got an impossible, unprecedented case. Maybe we're just talking about stress, burnout. You know, performance anxiety."

"Hardly," Jacob muttered. If anything, his dream performance was way beyond anything he'd done in the waking world—and, if his partners were to be believed, he was no slouch in that department.

"Not that kind of performance," Aaron said, waving away the comment. "Dreams are your subconscious mind speaking to your consciousness. Unfortunately, dreams don't speak English. They speak in symbols. You're fixated on this case. She's a problem to solve; a mystery to unlock. You're dreaming of having sex with her. That suggests that you've 'buried' yourself in the case. You would represent the key, she would represent the lock. Sex as unlocking."

Jacob grimaced. "Why the fuck wouldn't I just dream about a key?"

"Not as fun?" Aaron said, chuckling. "Who knows? The thing is, your subconscious speaks in weird ways. If you're dreaming about her this often, your subconscious may have a clue to the cure that you can't seem to puzzle out when you're awake."

"*Huh . . .*" Jacob liked the sound of that, feeling immediately better. Then he frowned. "These aren't like any dreams I've had before, Aaron. They're unbelievably real." His mind flashed to his last interlude with Rory, his body arching in to hers, his muscles bunching as he found release. "They're as real as anything I've ever felt when I'm awake."

Maybe even more real.

Aaron frowned. "Maybe you should describe the dreams to me."

"In detail?" Jacob said, aghast.

"Don't worry, I'm not looking for a play-by-play," Aaron reassured him. "Just set the scene. Maybe there are other symbols you're missing."

"I'm in a luxurious resort," Jacob said, closing his eyes and shifting to that dream environment as easily as conjuring up a picture of Aaron's apartment. "It's on a tropical island somewhere. The resort itself looks like a castle. There's a high tower, and I know there's a luxury suite up there. That's where I find her. There's no one else in the place but her."

"Asleep in the tower," he murmured. "Mythic."

Jacob suddenly smacked his forehead. "Sleeping Beauty."

"What?"

"That's what they've called her case." He laughed, feeling relief flood through his body. "That's why she's in a castle. In a tower. I've been calling her 'Sleeping Beauty' since I heard about her!"

Aaron smiled. "See? It's nothing to worry about."

"God. You have no idea how much better I feel." Jacob stood up, stretching out. "I was starting to feel like I was losing my mind. I mean, I was beginning to go to bed earlier and earlier, just to see her. I was starting to think—"

He stopped, abruptly realizing how much he was revealing.

"Starting to think what?" Aaron's eyes were fixed on Jacob.

"It's dumb," Jacob muttered. "I mean, it just felt . . . real."

"You were starting to think *she* was real," Aaron reiterated.

Jacob shrugged uncomfortably.

Aaron was silent for a long moment. Then he cleared his throat. "You know, maybe your sex dreams are just a way of saying it's time you got laid."

Jacob forced a laugh, knowing his brother was just trying to lighten the situation. "It has been awhile."

"My professional recommendation would be to start relaxing more. Get a hobby. Get lucky. Get a life." Aaron winked, and Jacob's laugh was more relaxed. "Being this fixated on a case, any case, is going to be detrimental to your performance as a doctor."

Jacob nodded, a broad smile on his face. "Thanks, little brother. I guess this psychiatry isn't such a bogus science, after all."

Aaron normally rose to the bait when Jacob made pot-shots about his profession, but now he simply shrugged. "I will suggest also that if you still have the dreams, you try talking to *her*. Like I said, the subconscious works in weird and mysterious ways. This could be a roundabout way for it to tell you something important."

Jacob rolled his eyes. "Got it."

"One other thing," and Aaron's voice was solemn as he said it, "if you're still having the dreams in two weeks—or you start to feel like she's 'real' again—I want you to call me."

"Why?" Jacob felt discomfort creep over his skin. He laughed again, the sound more forced than before. "What, should I be worried or something?"

Aaron didn't answer, and Jacob suddenly realized . . . Aaron was already worried.

Just a dream. Ask her what she's there to tell me. Just my subconscious. Just a dream.

Jacob fell asleep, chanting the statements to himself. When he saw the familiar room, he felt a chill of apprehension go through him.

Bright sunlight flooded through the open French doors, letting in the balmy tropical breeze. Rory sat at a small table, reading a book, wearing only a light silk robe in a sumptuous slate blue that complimented her eyes. When she saw him, the book immediately closed, and she sprang to her feet, rushing to him.

"Jacob." Her arms looped around his neck, and she kissed

him steadily, her robe falling open as she pressed her body against his.

Jacob gritted his teeth as his body began its instantaneous reaction to her closeness. He inhaled her sweet, flowery scent. Gently but firmly, he disengaged her from him. "Rory," he said slowly, "what are you here to tell me?"

"What?" She stared at him blankly. "Tell you? What do you mean?"

"Why am I dreaming about you?"

With that, her look of puzzlement melted into an expression of delight. "You dream about me?" She toyed with the buttons on his shirt, allowing the folds of her robe to part as she did so. Tantalizing glimpses of flesh were revealed, then covered, as the silk whispered around her body. "What do you dream?"

He grasped her hand, with slightly more pressure than he intended, wiping the smile from her face. "I'm dreaming now," he said. "*This* is a dream. This isn't real."

"A dream? This is a dream?" She tugged her hand away. Her gray eyes looked haunted. "I suppose it makes sense. I'd wondered . . . but of course. This *is* a dream."

Somehow, her hesitant confirmation didn't make him feel better. If anything, he felt worse—because she was so obviously crestfallen. Could you disappoint a figment of your imagination? Worse, you could ruin her sense of identity?

"You're my subconscious," he continued relentlessly. "I'm obviously focusing on you because I think you'll provide me with some answer or solution to the problem I'm having—"

"Wait," she said, holding up her hand to stop him. "You're saying I'm *your* dream?"

"Naturally." Her reaction made no sense to him.

Then she laughed, shocking him even further. "I didn't see that one coming. Especially from a guy who just appears and vanishes in front of me."

It took him a second to figure out what she was saying. Finally, he gaped at her. "You're saying you think I'm in *your* dream?"

"No, I *know* you're in my dream," she countered. "So I don't know what you expect me to tell you."

He rubbed at his temples with his fingertips. Aaron was going to laugh his butt off at this turn of events.

She smiled again, her eyes still wary even though her face shone with forced brightness. "Well, since we're both in agreement that this is a dream . . ."

She reached for his belt buckle. He dodged stubbornly, and she frowned.

"What? What's the matter?"

"I'm not here to have sex," he said, even as his muscles practically screamed in protest. Just the luscious shadow of her cleavage, displayed between the open neckline of her robe, was enough to have his mouth watering. "I'm here to get some answers."

Her eyes glowed with a silent anger. "Fine," she replied softly.

Then she dropped the robe, letting the silk fall and pool at her feet. The gold-kissed ivory of her skin gleamed in the morning sun. With the utmost casualness, she strode across the thick carpet to the suite's small sitting area. She chose a chair opposite a small divan. Crossing her legs, she sat, surveying him, her nipples proudly jutting out. Her chin lifted.

"What, exactly, did you want to know?"

Now his mouth went dry. His fingers itched to touch all that exposed skin. He could still smell her . . . still feel her, under his palms, over his cock. He suppressed a tremor.

Clearing his throat, he decided to play her game. He sat across from her, on the suite's plush sofa.

"Remember when I told you I was a neurologist? I'm *your* doctor," he said, and he forced every word out as sharply as he could. "You've been in a coma for six years."

"What?" Her expression had been sarcastic, taunting. Now her face showed only dismay. "What did you say?"

"Coma. You've been asleep for six years, ever since taking a Caribbean vacation after graduating from college. Which I assume accounts for the location of this dream."

His voice was coldly detached. Clinical.

She looked as if he'd struck her. She stared at him, eyes wide, body slumped in the chair. Her legs parted unconsciously as she leaned forward, her head in her hands.

He shouldn't have noticed, but he couldn't help it. The way her breasts swung, gently enticing. The golden curls that shielded her sex, parting to reveal the slightest suggestion of the treasure beyond. His cock tautened and shifted, like a predator tensing for imminent pursuit.

Then she looked up. Her eyes were glossy with unshed tears.

"Rory." Instead of acting on his needs, he was at her side, kneeling next to her, feeling contrite. Which was stupid.

This is still just a dream!

"Six years?" she breathed. "I felt like I'd been dreaming for so long, but I had no idea . . ."

She was speaking as though she were a real person. How had his subconscious created this persona? And how could he resist her?

Stay focused, he counseled himself, even as his arm went around her naked shoulders. Her skin, normally so hot, felt cool to the touch. He clutched her to him, and she hugged him tightly, without seduction.

"What's the last thing you remember?" he whispered against her ear.

She went still. "I was . . . with Oliver."

Funny how he bristled at the sound of another man's name in her mouth. "What happened when you were with Oliver?" he forced himself to ask, even as his jaw clenched.

"I was going to have sex with him." Now it was her turn to sound clinical. She scooted away from him, looking at him curiously. "But I didn't."

"You didn't want to?" Was that hope in his voice?

"I did want to," she said. "But not because it was him."

He frowned.

"I wanted to because I'd never had sex before," she clarified. "Oliver had been asking me out for years. He was good-looking, had a decent reputation. He worshiped the ground I walked on." She smiled sadly. "And I knew that once he'd had me, he'd move on without pestering me for a relationship. He wasn't a bad man, that's just the way he was, and that was exactly what I needed."

A strange mix of feelings washed over Jacob. Anger and jealousy led the pack, incensed that someone else had touched her, or tried to. Then relief that she hadn't been attached emotionally to the guy. Then puzzlement—both at the fact that he was relieved and then because of her last observation. "Why wouldn't you want a relationship?"

"I wanted a relationship," she said. "Just not with him."

"So . . . why didn't you wait to have sex with someone you did want to have a relationship with?"

She stared at him. Then she laughed, with an edge of bitterness.

"Because you hadn't shown up," she said. "And I guess I was beginning to doubt you ever would."

He felt a warm protectiveness curl in the pit of his stomach. "I'm sure I'm not the only man who would've been a good match for you," he said, even as every fiber of his being protested the statement. *No man would be better for you . . .*

"Have you had a relationship with every woman you've ever slept with?"

He sighed. "Point taken. So what happened? What caused the coma?"

"I don't know."

"You must have some idea . . ."

"I don't know." Her voice shook. "One moment, I was there, in the bed . . . then I remember going numb. I couldn't move. I couldn't speak. Then everything went black."

"And then?"

She shifted, and he felt the heat of her body, seeping through the light cotton of his shirt . . . warming his khaki slacks. "Then I woke up here. And I've woken up here every morning since that day."

"You sleep?" The words came out strained, as her breast brushed against his arm.

She nodded. "I'm the only one at this hotel. When I first got here, I explored a bit. There was no one else. Here, I mean."

There was something about the way she paused, the strange feel to that last sentence, that made him want to ask a question, but she turned to face him more squarely, and he was sidetracked by the view and her proximity.

"So I spend my days reading books I've found in various rooms. I work out in the hotel gym, or spend time in the spa. I meditate." She shrugged. "I just killed time, until you woke me up."

She leaned forward, kissing him tenderly. He kissed her back, leaning into her, their mouths smoothly dancing over each other in a soft, melting caress.

"When you showed up, you were all I could think about," she murmured, her voice a hot lash against his skin. "When you made love to me, I didn't need anything else."

He shivered. When she reached for the buttons of his shirt, he didn't stop her.

She slid the material off his shoulders, and he shrugged out of it, leaning back to give her access to his fly. She undid the button, unzipping the rest quickly, easing the waistband off of him. He stood, and she stripped off the rest of his clothes.

Soon, he was just as naked as she was. She stood, meeting him—matching him.

"Take me," she pleaded, dragging her erect nipples against his chest. Then she reached down, the skin of her palms soft as water as she circled the hard, hot flesh of his cock. He groaned, pressing against her grip. She stroked her finger over the tiny hole at the tip of his cock head, gathering a drop of wetness as his body strained against his constraints. He watched as she put her finger up to her lips, her rosy tongue darting out like a cat's to taste it.

He had to have her. *Now.*

Even the bed was too far. He tugged her to the divan, his heart pounding, his body nuclear with the heat. He sat, reaching for her hips, guiding her until she was straddling him. Her legs were on either side of his thighs, putting her deliciously full breasts at eye level. He suckled, and she whimpered, squirming, trying to lower herself on his cock. He felt her wet curls brush against his cock head.

He reached between her legs, stroking the slick folds of her, rolling against her clit in the way he'd learned she most liked. As she gasped, he penetrated with one finger as he bit gently on the side of one of her breasts.

She cried out, her body shivering with orgasm, and he pressed hot kisses on her ribcage and her stomach as his fingers withdrew. "I'm obsessed with you," he admitted in a hoarse whisper. "I shouldn't want you this way."

"You can have me this way," she breathed, "or any other way you want me."

He paused, on the brink of entering her.

"Jacob," she said insistently, rocking her hips. He felt the slick skin of her pussy brush against his cock head.

He relented, guiding her down on his cock, parting the way with his hand as his bluntness pressed inside her. She lowered herself completely, taking him in fully, until their stomachs molded against one another and their chests touched.

"Rock against me," he ordered.

She did as he told her, her legs wrapping around his waist as she tilted her head back, her hips moving in a rhythmic motion. She moaned softly. He nudged her with his fingertips until she followed, lifting herself gently, then he coaxed her back down, angling her slightly, moving her in a steady cycle of deep thrusts. At one point, she gasped, and he recognized he'd found what he was looking for. He moved, more insistently, making sure his cock hit that special spot.

She screamed in ecstasy when the second orgasm rolled through her, and he felt the hot wetness flood over his cock, drenching his balls. His smile was triumphant.

No one else could ever, will ever, make her feel like this.

Now it was his turn. He stood, and she let out a little gasp of surprise when he placed her against the cool, smooth wall. He buried his head in the crook of her neck, flexing, his hips thrusting as he penetrated her even more deeply. She moaned and cried out, arching her pelvis to meet his every urgent, powerful penetration.

"That's it, baby, that's right," he muttered, feeling the beginnings of his own orgasm begin to creep through him. "Come on. Come for me."

"Jacob," she breathed. They were mating like animals, clutching each other in a frenzy of desire. When he felt her clench around him, he shouted, finally succumbing to release. The orgasm tore through him like a shotgun blast, and his cock shuddered inside her as she clutched him, her hips jolting against his in involuntary spasms.

He could barely bring them to the bed before they both collapsed on it, his cock still buried inside her.

"You could do that to me for the rest of my life," she finally murmured, her voice sleepy with satisfaction. "I don't need anything else but you."

He found himself nodding, thinking: *This is perfect. This is paradise.*

But this wasn't paradise. It wasn't even real.

Chapter Four

Rory waited in her room, impatient. Jacob would return. He always did.

He had to.

He materialized out of nowhere, just as he had for weeks now. And just like she had since the first day she'd seen him, she felt a searing desire to touch him, to be touched *by* him. She wanted to feel him inside her. She wanted . . .

No. This wasn't about desire.

This was about answers.

"Rory," he greeted her with a groan.

"I'm not just a dream," Rory said quickly. "I mean . . . I might be in a dream, but I'm not just a figment of your imagination."

She watched as Jacob sat next to her on the bed. Her stomach tightened with the now-familiar need, but she ignored it. This was too important for her, and it needed to be addressed, even if every nerve in her body was screaming *touch him, taste him, take him . . .*

He stared at her. "What do you need to tell me, Rory?"

"Stop saying that." She picked up a pillow, hurling it at him in rage.

He ignored it. "You're obviously here for a reason," he said, his voice patient—patronizing. "I want to heal you."

"I know," she said, with a trace of bitterness. "I'm *the case*, as you put it."

At least he looked embarrassed. "I'm sorry about that," he said. "I get very involved in my work. It was before I knew you . . ." Then he grimaced. "Although, technically, I suppose I still don't really know you, since you're not . . ."

"Tell me, do you usually get this involved?" she asked, her voice sharp. "Do you always dream about sleeping with your patients, Doctor White?"

With that, he stood up, his face pale and drawn. "I have *never* touched a patient inappropriately. I've never done *anything* that might jeopardize someone's well-being, physically or otherwise." His voice shook with fury. "And no, I've never felt this way about anyone I've treated. Not even in dreams."

He sounded incensed, truly pained, and she immediately realized that she'd wounded him far more than she'd intended. She took a tentative step toward him, her hand reaching out to comfort him. "I'm sorry," she murmured.

He shied away. "Don't," he cautioned.

She felt even worse. Reluctantly, she put her hand down.

"You're different," he admitted, finally. "The first time I saw you, I couldn't believe how beautiful you were. You looked so peaceful, and I thought, it's so damned *unfair* that you were trapped in this state—comatose. That you'd lost so much time. And even though I know it's a long shot, and I know that you're not going to help my career and that there isn't even anything I can do for you . . . I couldn't be rational. I had to help you, no matter what."

He stared at her, his blue eyes tortured. Her body still wanted him, but it was her heart that reacted to his impassioned speech.

"When I saw you here, touched you, and I realized it was a dream, I couldn't help myself," he admitted in a tortured whisper.

"I'm glad," she breathed, taking a step closer to him, but he held up a hand in warning.

"I'm not," he ground out. "It's making it too difficult in the real world. I wake up, and I see you . . . and I'm worried that I'm going to lose my judgment. And I *won't* do that. But . . ." He looked at her, hungrily, helplessly. "I don't know what to do."

She felt her body tighten with need. She reached for him, ignoring his tension and the anxiety written on his face. She pressed her body against his.

"This is a dream," she agreed. "You're a good man. You won't do anything I don't want you to do. This is our place."

He looked haunted by her words. She decided talk had no further place and stood up on tiptoes, pressing a kiss against his lips.

He stood frozen for the longest moment of her life, then, with a harsh cry, he leaned down and kissed her, his lips punishing hers in a rough kiss. She gasped against his onslaught, reveling in the searing sensation of his passion. "Yes," she breathed, as he shifted his attention to her neck, suckling sharp little love bites of pleasure against her sensitive skin. She shed her garment, wondering absently why she even bothered with the thing—or why he bothered with clothes, if this were a dream. They were here because their bodies called to each other.

She was starting to believe she existed only to answer the siren call of his body's sensual invitation.

"Wait, no," he said, tearing himself away, and she felt an edge of frustration, coupled with a profound sadness. "You need to tell me why you're here."

"For *fuck's* sake," she spat out. "I don't *know* why I'm here!"

He grimaced in pain, holding her at arm's length. "You're here to tell me what I need to know," he explained. "You must be. I've been dreaming about you every night. You must have some key—some cure. Something I've been overlooking in all the files and all the data."

"Are you kidding me?" Anger snapped through her. "You really think that I'm just some . . . some representation of your subconscious, don't you? You still think I'm not real!"

He sighed. "I want to make love to you until I'm blind," he said, with a tone of regret. "But . . . you're becoming an obsession, Rory. I need to ask you what it is you need to tell me."

"I'm not just some part of you," she protested, the heat of her desire fueling the fire of her anger. "I'm real, Jacob. I'm *Rory*. If anything, you're in *my* dream."

He laughed bitterly. "That's not possible."

"How do you know?"

"Fine. We'll play it your way," he said, crossing his arms. "Tell me something about yourself that only you would know. Something that I couldn't have learned from my files."

She opened her mouth, then shut it. "How am I supposed to know what you've read?"

"You can't answer because I don't really know much about you, Rory," he answered, his voice inarguable. "And, since you're a part of me, you only know what I know."

"I'm . . . not real." The thought made her feel panicked, scared. Sick to her stomach. She sat down on the bed again.

He sighed again, then sat next to her, enfolding her in his arms. "I'm sorry," he said, his voice far more gentle.

"I feel real," she countered. "What I feel for you—that feels real, too."

He closed his eyes, resting his forehead against hers. "What I feel for you," he said, his voice low, "is . . ."

He trailed off. "Inappropriate?" she asked, with a trace of bitterness.

"What I feel for you is more than I've ever felt for anyone," he said instead. "And I don't know why. I don't know you. I've never spoken to you. You're beautiful—but it's more than that. How can it be more than that?" He opened his eyes, his sky blue eyes staring into her face as if he were studying her soul. "Why you?"

"I don't have any answers for you, Jacob. Not even for that."
She kissed his cheek, then his lips. "But I understand."

They sat like that, quiet for a long moment. Then, they
kissed again, slowly and with great tenderness.

When he stripped off his shirt, it was with a casual grace
that was nothing like the hurried, almost frantic, joining
they'd experienced in the pool. He was infinitely gentle with
her. Even though her body was aflame with desire, she was
in no rush, preferring to linger over the details of his body,
knowing that he was giving in to this passion despite his res-
ervations. She didn't understand what was happening, but
in this moment, she didn't care. She simply wanted to enjoy
him, to somehow give him a balm for his wounded and tortured conscience.

She wanted to love him.

Suddenly, a tendril of fear curled up through the ripples of
desire, and she pushed the thought out of her mind.

He slipped out of his clothes easily, then sat side by side
with her on the oval bed. He stroked her hair, then her face,
then her shoulders and her back. She traced the pectoral
muscles on his chest, the ripples of his abdomen, the cut of
muscle at his hips. He smoothed his palms over her breasts.
She played with the length of his arousal, growing longer and
harder with each passing stroke.

He leaned down to tease her lips with his, his tongue darting around the soft inner skin of her lips. She teased back,
her tongue tickling his as her hands continued to explore,
cupping the sliding globes of his balls before dragging her
nails lightly down his thighs. She didn't know how she knew

he'd like it, but he did, his cock nudging against her wrist. She laughed against his mouth, and felt his smile broaden against hers.

I love you.

Again, the thought followed with a sinking feeling of fear. She stretched out on her back, and he stretched out beside her, staring into her eyes, smiling. The pain and guilt that wracked his expression was slowly being erased with a joy that made her heart clench and her stomach dissolve into a sugary fire.

He reached down, his fingers playing with her labia, rolling the lips gently around her clitoris. She felt pleasure stab through her, and she arched her back, her hips pressing against the gentle exploration of his hand. Languorously, he sucked on her breast as he continued his lazy finger strokes. She parted her legs slightly, feeling his cock pressing blunt and damp against the outside of her thigh. She could feel heat suffuse through her system. She had been turned on before—a knee-jerk reaction to seeing him, she knew. But this was increasing her desire by degrees, turning her on with a slow intensity that was different than anything he'd shown her in the past. She breathed hard, writhing slightly as he suckled and caressed, stroked and nibbled.

She felt the beginnings of orgasm start to shimmer through her, and she gasped as it rolled over her, causing her to shudder against his steadily working fingertips. When she recovered, she looked up to find him smiling at her, his eyes filled with delight. She smiled back at him, her muscles relaxing in a languid mass.

He rolled her over, massaging the muscles of her back in a way that had her purring like a cat in the sun. *"Ooh,* just a bit lower," she said, as he worked at a knot just over her sacrum. He did as she instructed, then she felt his hand stray back between her legs.

"This low?" he asked playfully.

"You found the spot," she joked back, lifting her buttocks slightly in invitation.

She quickly gasped when she felt his penis head stroking against her slick opening. She let out a surprised laugh that quickly disappeared when he entered her, shallowly penetrating her, then retreating.

"Like that?" he asked. His voice was lower, huskier.

"Mmm-hmm," she responded, and was gratified when he entered her again, a short, slow, thorough plumb of her depths. He angled slightly, twisting his hips so that his cock turned and stroked in a delicate ring about an inch inside her. She felt an unexpected shock of pleasure, and tightened her muscles around him. He growled in response, pressing in a little deeper, then retreating.

She shifted, her hand working its way down her body until she found her still throbbing clit. She stroked it as he entered her, feeling a delicious glow of pleasure radiating through her. He noticed, and made a noise of approval.

"That's it, sweetheart," he murmured, his rhythm altering slightly, speeding up just a touch, then slowing. He moved with patient deliberation, first shallow, then deep, then shallow again. She wriggled against him, her hips backing up to meet him. She made incoherent noises of pleasure as his hips worked their magic.

The second orgasm was a slower, more powerful echo of the first, and she cried out his name, her cunt milking him with its powerful contractions. He went still, and she felt the tension of every muscle bunched against hers. Still, he didn't give in to the temptation.

Instead, he withdrew, nudging her to roll over. She did, and he lifted her gently, having her straddle his lap. "I want to see your face this time," he said, kissing the tip of her nose, and she felt immensely, absurdly touched. She lowered herself on his wet, hard cock, and for a moment, they remained like that, their bodies joined but still, her breasts crushed against his chest, her legs twined around his waist. Then, with a dancer's grace, they started to move together. She flexed her hips, raising and lowering herself on his massive, engorged cock, loving the sensation of him filling her, dragging his hard shaft against her still-quivering clit. Her fingers dug into his shoulders, her thighs clenching tight around his hips as he arched and angled, pulling her hips flush against him as he penetrated her fully. "Oh God, Rory," he murmured, his tempo picking up. His face was strained, dark with passion, and his breathing was ragged.

She gasped against him, her hips moving quickly, meeting his with every stroke, every thrust. She wanted everything he could give her. She felt gloriously, deliciously alive.

"Rory!" he shouted, slamming against her.

She felt the third orgasm flood her and she cried out, cling-ing to him like a drowning woman as her senses exploded around her. She could feel his cock shuddering inside her as her pussy clenched in tight circles around him. She threw back her head, her body shaking as the overwhelming cas-cade of sensations threatened to make her black out.

They stayed like that, holding each other tight, kissing each other with soft, almost sobbing breaths. Finally, he rolled them onto the bed, still joined. He pushed a sweaty lock of hair out of her eyes. His look of adoration was one she couldn't understand, but one she desperately wanted to believe was sincere.

I love you.

But no—she couldn't say that. She couldn't remember why—but she couldn't, wouldn't admit that, not even to him.

You shouldn't have made love to her again, he chastised him-self. He disengaged from her, rolling away from her on the large bed. Her eyes looked wounded at his action.

"What do you have to tell me?" he repeated.

She winced. "Really?" She asked in a soft voice. "You're still going to keep pestering me about that?"

"I'm here to cure you. I keep dreaming about you—here, with this. I can't keep this up. Not without it affecting my work."

"Your work." Her voice was both doubtful and derisive. "Well. God forbid something like a relationship with me gets in the way of your work."

"Relationship? What relationship? You're not even real!" His back stiffened. "You've either got to have something to help me, or I'm going to stop seeing you."

"You would stop seeing me?" She went pale as parchment. "After . . . after what we've done?"

" 'We' haven't done anything. You're not even here. You're just a few misfirings of my neurons," he said coldly. "So yes, if you're not serving any useful purpose, I won't continue dreaming of you."

He knew it was probably a lie as he said it—*Can I even help dreaming about her?*—but he stood firm, willing himself to be convincing.

She sat up, crossing her arms over her chest, not in defiance but in a crushing gesture to her vulnerability. She reached for the sheet, draping it around herself as if she were cold. The room suddenly darkened as clouds crossed over the sun.

"You're my doctor," she said tentatively. "You're going to wake me up."

He nodded curtly.

"And that's really more important than . . ." She made a strangled sound, gesturing to the bed. "This? Us?"

"It's my life," he said. "You're a case. An important case. And I'd devote my life to curing you."

"For your reputation," she said bitterly.

He shrugged. "It will help my reputation, without question. But no, it's not the most important consideration."

"Then what is the most important consideration?"

You, he wanted to say, but he was too raw, too close to losing it. *She's not real*, he repeated to himself. If he lost sight of that, he'd get even more lost in this subconscious world of his.

And what would that do to him when he woke up? How would it affect the life that actually *counted*?

"The important part is the challenge," he found himself saying instead. "I can't just sit by passively. When I take up a challenge, I do whatever I have to do to meet it."

"I see." She sat there, silent.

"Which is why I know you're my subconscious," he found himself expanding. "If you were really here—trapped in some dreamland environment—wouldn't you be trying to figure out a way to wake up? But no. You're just here, reading, entertaining yourself. Killing time."

Her eyes snapped with indignation. "And what was I supposed to be doing? Building signal fires?"

"At least that would be something," he retorted, unsure of why he was attacking her. Or, considering she was simply an aspect of his alter ego, why he was attacking himself. "Instead, you're just . . . you're just *taking* it. Why haven't you done something?"

"There's more on this island than the resort," she said darkly. "Believe me, there are things you'd never want to see."

"If I thought they'd cure you," he answered, "I'd face them. And if you wanted out of here, you'd help me."

"So you're calling me a coward?" She bristled.

"I'm saying I'm not sure you really want to wake up."

She bounded off the bed, turning on him, the sheet wrapped around her like a shield. "How dare you—"

Blackness. A sudden snap. Suddenly, he was staring at Carrie the night nurse. "Again?" he said.

She nodded, looking worried. "Yes. Worse, this time. Something different's happening."

Throwing on a robe, he followed her to Rory's room. Rory's color was hectic, her brain waves still moving . . . still swaying.

He was actually witnessing it this time.

"If she's capable of this," he murmured with growing excitement, "she could wake up. She's got the potential. There's not much damage . . ."

"Do you really think so, Doctor?"

He hadn't meant to say it aloud, but now that he had, he realized he meant it. "Yes. Absolutely."

"Do you know what's causing it, then? The improvement?"

He looked down at Rory's face. Instead of its usual serene, expressionless visage, she seemed to be . . .

Frowning.

Just as he'd seen her, just moments before.

He felt a cold chill wash over him. He ignored it.

"No," he finally answered Carrie, with a trace of uneasiness. "I still have no idea."

Rory stood in her room, hugging herself lightly. Jacob had disappeared.

She was still stinging from his accusations. Flinching at each remembered word.

You're just taking it. Why haven't you done something?

She grimaced, closing her eyes. Then she let out a long, frustrated scream.

"Do you think I like being here?" She picked up a pillow from the couch, throwing it out on the balcony. "Years! I've been trapped on this island for *years!* Do you think that, if there were a way I could wake up, I wouldn't have *done* it by now?"

She pummeled the couch, beating it with increasing force until she was exhausted. She finally collapsed, feeling hot, angry tears crawling down her cheek. She brushed them away with the back of her hand, fury still pulsing through her.

As the fury receded, she started to notice the guilt.

Have you done everything you could? Really?

She got up, putting on her clothes. She left her room, heading for the kitchen. She could walk these halls blindfolded. At one point or another, she had investigated every single room. The place held no secrets for her. It was, for better or worse, her home.

Had she gotten comfortable? She had thought of it as acceptance. Like Robinson Crusoe, she had made the best of her surroundings. In a Zenlike way, she'd adapted to her prison by fully enjoying moments: books, cooking in the kitchen, the bubbling heat of the hot tubs. She had used a journal to process and document her solitude. She had meditated.

She had slept without dreaming.

Then, in her solitary world, a man had suddenly appeared, like magic . . . and the way he'd touched her was beyond her comprehension. To a woman starving for any interaction, their lovemaking was not only a lifeline, but a miracle. No wonder she hadn't questioned his appearances. They were too important to her sanity.

Now, he was dismissing her as a part of his subconscious—and worse, issuing ultimatums about her usefulness.

She had never been a violent person before. But then, he seemed to bring out all sorts of baser urges in her.

"He thinks I'm not doing anything?" She pushed open the glass doors of the lobby with a fierce shove. "He has no idea."

With anger fueling her, she strode out of the hotel, past its manicured lawns and well-kept shrubbery. She kept walking until the vegetation grew thicker, wilder. The trees grew together, thick and unkempt, blocking out the sun. It grew progressively darker. She was moving away from the "safe" side of the island—the touristy, moneyed area. She was moving past the native ghetto, a smaller version of Jamaica's Trenchtown. She had no fear of this place: she had been here, early on. The ramshackle shanties and poor lodgings were empty. Like the hotel, this, too, was abandoned.

It wasn't until she got past all hallmarks of any kind of civilization that fear began to push past her fury. Warning signals danced along her nervous system. Determined, she pushed her way through the underbrush, ignoring the harsh beating of her heart. She blamed her sweat on the blast-furnace-hot humidity rather than on the heat of her body's own trepidation.

She heard the sounds she could still remember, even

though it had been years since she'd last heard them. Drum beats, loud and tribal. Grunting chants. She forced herself to keep walking toward the source of the commotion.

She finally reached her destination. The trees grew so tall and thick that they blocked out all light. The drumbeat hit a frenzied pitch. She crept forward, hiding behind a large rock. The air was thick with the smells of incense, hibiscus, and rum. The voices were loud and incoherent. She peered out, careful not to be noticed. Her heart threatened to beat right out of her chest.

The figures were human—and yet, not. A tall man in somber clothing with a tall black hat stood, not drumming or chanting, but merely looking bored. An old man hobbled around with a cane, his eyes light and mischievous and deceptively young. A man writhed on the ground like a snake as a gorgeous woman in a multicolored gossamer dress danced over him.

They were performing some kind of ritual. There were symbols drawn on the ground in poured salt. And in the center of it all was a woman, tall and beautiful and fierce looking, with deep chocolate skin and long black braids. She was chanting loudly, throwing herbs on the fire that produced thin strings of acrid black smoke. "Legba, open the door to the next world," she instructed the older man, and he nodded, doing a surprisingly spry dance around the symbol.

The woman then gestured to two young muscular men, one blond, one dark haired.

"I channel the *loa* Erzuli," the woman said. "She needs pleasing. She needs feeding."

"Yes, Serafina." The men smiled, obviously happy with the request. Slowly, they peeled off their shirts and jeans, until they were standing naked before the woman.

The woman—Serafina—smiled back, a royal smile of satisfaction. "You'll do," she said, with a hint of condescension. "You'll serve." With that, she reached up, taking off her own dress. Her body was perfect, as if carved from onyx.

The drumming continued. The other people did not move, though they did not look away. If anything, they seemed interested in the goings-on.

Rory felt emotions churn through her. On some level, she was horrified by what she was watching—and at the same time, she felt a strange, terrible fascination running through her. She wanted to look away. *How will this help me wake up?*

What's worse, she knew what had happened last time . . . and she did not want to witness a repeat of that episode.

The woman stroked first one man's chest, then the other. The men seemed spellbound by her touch. There was something absent about their eyes, Rory noticed, as if they were soulless. Nonetheless, they moved eagerly at the woman's instruction.

The woman leaned her head back, her eyes closing halfway, revealing only the whites of her eyes. She began chanting in an unfamiliar tongue. It must have been some sort of instruction. When she finished, the men caressed her breasts and hips, murmuring something incoherent, stroking her with intent. She continued her incantation. Then she stood, somehow taller and even more regal.

"Erzuli is here."

Her voice seemed otherworldly. She also seemed somehow more beautiful—and more frightening.

She kissed first the blond man, her tongue twining with his. Then the dark-haired man. They moved closer to her, their cocks standing out like jousting poles. She stroked her hand over first one penis, then the other, alternating, teasing one with her fingertips as she kissed the other. They swayed against her, moaning softly.

They seemed more animal than human . . . all of them.

The woman snapped her fingers, and her men moved reluctantly away from her, pulling out a blanket. They spread the blanket over the symbol, then stretched out on it. She looked at them like a woman at a banquet, deciding what to sample first.

Then, she joined them on the blanket—but they were the ones that feasted.

The blond focused on her breasts, taking first one dark nipple, then the other into his mouth as her fingers twined in his hair. The dark-haired man went between her thighs, nibbling on them, then focusing on her pussy, lapping at it industriously, his fingers burrowing between her luxurious curls.

"Serafina," the blond man murmured, licking at her areola with quick, whiplike flicks of his tongue. "Serafina."

The dark-haired man groaned, his mouth open, his tongue darting in and out of her. She leaned back, smiling indulgently. Her nipples were red, erect, wet with the blond's insistent suckling. She sighed, her hips lifting up off the blanket to meet the dark man's hunger. Her breathing quickened, her hips starting to gyrate. The dark-haired man held tight as the blond started stroking and massaging her breasts. She covered the blond's hands with her own, squeezing her breasts as her hips rocked frantically. Then she cried out, a throaty, rippling sound of satisfaction.

Rory leaned against the boulder, hoping that this meant it was over. She was confused by what she was seeing. She was also, she hated to admit, strangely aroused, her pussy starting to pulse disturbingly.

They weren't finished. The woman, "Serafina," changed position, getting on all fours. The blond took position behind her, the dark-haired man in front of her. The blond penetrated her, his long cock disappearing between her legs as she moaned in appreciation. She reached out, then took the dark-haired man's cock in her mouth. The men closed their eyes, swaying and rocking into her. She arched and flexed, backing up against the cock penetrating her, taking the other deeper into her mouth.

The assembled people watching swayed, too, almost unconsciously. Even Rory found her body moving restlessly. She held her chest, her arms crossed tightly, her thighs pressed together like a vise. She felt energy start to course through her, unexpectedly, and struggled to focus.

The men were getting close, sweat beading on their chests and foreheads. The dark-haired man was spasmodically clenching and unclenching his hands, breathing hard, his neck muscles bulging with strain. The blond started to pick up the pace, his fingers digging into Serafina's hips as he started to thrust inside her with more speed, more force.

Serafina released the dark-haired man, causing him to groan in disappointment. She snapped again. The blond stopped immediately, whimpering.

"Not this way," she said imperiously. "This is about my pleasure . . . Erzuli's pleasure." She lay back, her legs splayed enough that Rory could see the red flesh of her pussy. "I want you both, now." She turned onto her side, looking at them expectantly.

The men stretched out on either side of Serafina. She kissed the blond in front of her, crushing her breasts against his chest, stroking his penis. The dark-haired man spooned behind her, stroking his penis against her buttocks and the small of her back, his eyes half lidded. The blond man groaned against Serafina's lips, his hips moving forward, his cock pushing against her hand. She lifted her leg, hooking it over his hips. Rory could see both men's cocks poised at Serafina's cunt. The blond held her leg still, then shifted, pressing his cock up and inside her. He moaned, and Serafina growled with appreciation as the huge cock disappeared between her labia. The dark-haired man rocked behind her, pressed flush. The three writhed, their bodies stroking each other. The blond withdrew, and the dark-haired man eagerly took his place, sinking his cock in with force. They alternated, first one sex-heavy cock penetrating, then the other. When the dark-haired plunged in, the blond rubbed the tip of his cock against Serafina's clit as the other circled and gyrated against her. Serafina moved restlessly, gasping, stroking either man by turns, her hips swinging and rolling rhythmically. "Now," she bit out, her hips starting to piston with force.

The alternating stopped. The dark-haired man started to pound inside her as the blond stroked his cock against her clit purposefully. Their hips were a frenzy of movement, rubbing and stroking and licking each other, a cacophony of rasping breaths and jerky, hard contortions. The blond nipped at Serafina's breasts with an animallike grunt as the dark-haired man pummeled her with his hips. She met his every thrust eagerly. Finally, she shrieked with pleasure, her nails clawing down the blond's back, hard enough to leave bloody streaks. She shivered and shook. Then, breathless, she rolled over.

"Again?" the blond asked eagerly, stroking her breasts.

Serafina smiled. "Of course," she said dreamily. "We're not close to through yet." Then she tilted her head back— and her eyes locked with Rory's.

Rory gasped, diving behind the rock. Adrenaline flooded through her system, warning her to run, flee, before . . . before what? It was a dream . . . what could she possibly do to her?

"I can do worse things to you than you can imagine."

Rory held her breath. Then she glanced around the corner.

The woman was still looking at her, despite the eager mouths of her lovers. Serafina's smile was jagged, cruel.

"You should be thanking me on your knees that you have that fancy hotel," she said, her voice loud enough to carry to Rory's hiding place. "Be thankful that you're here, and not dead. I took pity on you."

"Why am I here?" Rory murmured.

"If you really want to know, this grove holds all the answers." The woman gasped briefly as the dark-haired man sucked particularly hard between her thighs. "But you've never wanted to know. You've always wanted to hide. And if you'd only stayed hidden, kept your curiosity intact, then you wouldn't be here."

Rory stepped cautiously toward the circle. The strange-looking nonhumans stared at her with curiosity, but no fear. Rory felt sick to her stomach but forced herself to continue taking step after step until she stood before the naked, mating mass.

"How can I leave?"

Serafina laughed harshly. "Leave?" She shook her head. "I said you could learn. I didn't say you could leave. You're trapped here."

"Forever?"

"Not forever." The woman twisted sinuously, stroking the blond's head tenderly. She laughed again. "Just until you die."

Rory felt as if she were in free fall. "That's not possible."

"You don't know what it would take," Serafina said. "There's power in you, but you refuse to use it. You've been here before—a long time ago."

Rory nodded, the nausea growing.

"You witnessed my ritual."

"Yes." Rory clutched her arms around herself.

"You saw me slaughter a simple goat, and that terrified you." Serafina looked dismissive. "There is power in blood. Just as there is power here."

"Here?"

"In sex." Serafina sat up slightly. The men were still suck-ing on her, still lathing her with their tongues. She seemed bored with it. "Sex is power. Power is everything."

"What about love?"

Serafina shook her head. "Love is weakness. It will get you nowhere."

"Then what about Jacob?"

Serafina's eyes narrowed. "Who?"

Suddenly, Rory realized she'd made a tactical error. Se-rafina, who seemed to know everything, didn't know about Jacob.

That meant there was a possibility.

That also meant she'd opened a door to danger that she hadn't even realized.

"You don't have to be so unhappy," Serafina said, her voice suddenly soft and alluring. "I have men to spare. You could enjoy yourself with them—and me. We could be powerful together. You could learn how to not only love this world, but control it."

Rory swallowed hard. The men finally stopped in their ministrations, disengaging long enough to look at her. Their chiseled bodies were sheer perfection—their faces like fallen angels. They stared at her hungrily.

"They know more about pleasure than any man you would ever meet in the waking world," Serafina offered. "And I know more about power than any man or woman."

"I . . . no. I won't."

Serafina shrugged. "Suit yourself," she said, then gestured to the men. They quickly went back to work.

Rory stared as the blond man moved forward, positioning himself between Serafina's thighs until his cock was at her entrance. Then he pushed forward. Serafina's smile was one of indulgent pleasure. The dark-haired man massaged her abundant breasts, then stroked his cock between the valley of her cleavage, his eyes closed.

Rory couldn't take it anymore. She turned and fled, up to the hotel . . . the only home she had left.

She could hear Jacob's voice in her head: *"I'm not sure you really want to wake up."*

She didn't stop running as tears poured down her cheeks. Now that she'd faced the dark part of the island, she wasn't sure if she really wanted to wake up, either.

"I need to ask you both a few questions," Jacob said carefully. "About Rory."

He was sitting in the same living room where he'd first met Mrs. Jacquard. He had been confident, then . . . arrogant. Now he felt bewildered, and in an increasing state of distress. Mrs. Jacquard must have been expecting it: she looked at him with a look of wistful acceptance and sad, quiet regret. Mr. Jacquard, on the other hand, looked away, as if furious but trying to mask it behind boredom.

"I don't know what else we can tell you," Mrs. Jacquard said, in her quiet voice. She was wearing another suit, this time a St. John's knit. His mother owned three, he thought absently. She always wore them when she left town for months at a time, when he was a child. "At least there's nothing I can tell you that you couldn't learn from the medical files."

"I want to know more about Rory as a person."

She blinked at him owlishly. "Why?"

Jacob leaned against the back of the armchair. "Because I'm trying to put together a picture of her life. I want to know what sort of influences she might have had that might have contributed to her condition. I need to know everything you could possibly tell me about her."

He'd taken hours to construct that lie. His voice was calm, but his palms sweated slightly as he recited the statement.

Mr. Jacquard looked bored. Mrs. Jacquard looked unconvinced.

Jacob sighed. "I just . . . I *need* to know, Mrs. Jacquard."

That was pure, sincere truth. She seemed to understand that, and nodded slowly.

"What can I tell you?" She leaned back, nervously fingering the ecru pearls on her necklace. "Rory was a wonderful child. Very happy, very healthy. A wonderful singer and a talented dancer. And smart! So smart. She graduated with honors from Vassar."

He nodded. "I read that in her files."

"She would have gone on to graduate school. She was thinking law." Mrs. Jacquard's voice was rich with pride. "Of course, she could have done anything she decided she wanted to do. Is this helping?"

"Keeping going," Jacob encouraged. "Please."

"What does this have to do with her state?" Mr. Jacquard interrupted sharply.

"Henri," Mrs. Jacquard said softly. "Please."

"Dear," he replied, and the casual venom in his voice made

the word no endearment, "I'm simply curious as to how this little trip down memory lane is going to help Doctor White get to the cause of her condition. That's all."

Jacob frowned at the man. "I don't know what I'm looking for, but I'm hoping I'll recognize it when I hear it. Anything at all might help."

"Well, then, you don't need me here." Mr. Jacquard stood, straightening his jacket. "I'm going to the club."

He strode out the door. Mrs. Jacquard looked at Jacob apologetically.

"It's still so hard on him," she said.

"What is?"

"Rory." She reached into her pocket, pulling out a linen handkerchief. She quickly caught the tears that were forming at the corners of her eyes. "He was always so protective of her. He never wanted her to go away for camp. She had to struggle with him to let her live on campus when she went to college. He couldn't protect her from this, and it tears him apart." She sniffled. "Tears us both apart."

He didn't know if that meant that she, too, was wrecked by Rory's condition—or if it meant that the marriage had been irrevocably damaged by their daughter's coma. Either statement appeared to be valid.

"He couldn't possibly have seen this coming," Jacob said, trying to calm her. "He can't protect her from something like this."

She shook her head, as if disagreeing with him, and she looked at him warily.

Jacob felt a prickle of apprehension.

"Could he?" Jacob whispered. "Did he have something to do with Rory's illness?"

Mrs. Jacquard sat up stiffly, seeming affronted—but there was something in her eyes that suggested he was right.

Mr. Jacquard had done something to his own daughter?

"My husband and I love Rory," she said sharply, and every word rang with sincerity. "We would never, *ever* do anything to hurt her. All we ever wanted was for her to be happy and safe. If you knew what we had to go through to get her . . ." She glared at him. "I took treatments, saw specialists, did *everything* to have Rory. And now you think this is somehow our fault?"

He hadn't said that she was involved. The fact that she said "our fault" suggested that she, too, might have something to hide. He sat at the edge of his seat, anger warring with wariness.

"Fertility treatments," he said calmly. "I'll have to do research on whether or not that could cause any detrimental future effects—"

"We didn't have her with fertility treatments," she answered. "We finally managed to have her ourselves."

"So you had Rory naturally?"

She hesitated. "Yes."

She's lying. Why was she lying? What had she done?

"Any childhood illnesses or injuries? Exposure to any contaminants?"

"Just what you've seen in the files," she said crisply. She still hadn't forgiven him for his accusation—and he was trying to calm her down enough to delve into the subject further, so he continued to act casually.

"She was a careful child, *hmm?*"

"Careful? No." Mrs. Jacquard's laugh sounded like a sob. "She was always reckless—but her heart was so kind, it often ran away with her."

Jacob nodded, encouraging her. He made a big show of taking out his notebook, jotting down a few notes. "A sweet child."

"Always befriended the one kid in school who seemed to have no friends," Mrs. Jacquard remembered. "Brought them over, gave her own toys to them."

"Generous." *How can I get this woman to admit what she's done to her own child?* Jacob's mind raced. "What else?"

"She brought home strays," Mrs. Jacquard said. "A kitten here, a turtle. Oh, the worst was when she was five. You won't believe what she brought home, injured from an alley."

Jacob suddenly dropped his pen. "A raccoon," he murmured.

"A . . . why, yes," she said, realizing he'd beaten her to the punch line. "How did you guess? Was it in the files?"

No. It wasn't. He felt a cold chill envelope his body.

"It must have been," he said. "Did the animal hurt her?"

"No. In fact, it behaved like a puppy with her." Mrs. Jacquard sighed. "Of course, we couldn't let her keep it . . . it could have given her rabies, or God knows what. But she loved it. Even named it. Mackie. I can't believe I remember that."

Jacob got up, picking up his pen with a hand that shook. He quickly tucked the pen in his pocket. "I'm sorry to have bothered you," he said. "I didn't mean to. I . . . I just thought I should know more about her."

"We never wanted to hurt her," Mrs. Jacquard repeated. "We only want her to be well. I have faith in you, Doctor White."

He nodded, then fled to his room.

He knew about Rory. His dream had told him about the raccoon . . . the name, all the details. Things that he had no earthly way of knowing.

What did it mean? Was he suddenly becoming prescient? Had he somehow gained ESP through sleep deprivation? Was he going crazy?

He blinked.

Or did that mean that Rory was real?

Chapter Five

When Jacob fell asleep that night, he arrived in Rory's room, just like always—only Rory wasn't there waiting for him. He was surprised, then he wasn't. Considering the way he'd left, he could barely expect her to welcome him with open arms, could he?

You're acting like she's real again.

He closed his eyes. The damned raccoon. How else could he have known about that strange detail?

"Rory?" he called, searching the room, then the suite. "Rory, please come out."

He started to feel concerned. He had to find her. He had to figure this out, test her.

Prove once and for all that she's not real.

He left the room, calling for her down the hallways. When he got downstairs and couldn't find her, his stomach began to clench, forming a ball of ice as fear stabbed through him. Was she hurt? Was she gone? Had he finally gotten his wish and banished her from his dreams for good?

If you're not useful, I won't keep dreaming about you.

Panic flooded his system. Even if she wasn't real, the thought of living without her touch, without her taste, was almost more than he could bear.

"Rory!" he yelled, rushing outside, scanning the grounds.

He saw her as she was walking up the pathway. She was weeping, looking frightened. When she saw him, she made a strained sob and ran for him. He opened his arms, and she rushed into his embrace. He clutched her frantically, holding her so tight it was a wonder she could breathe. "Rory," he whispered fiercely against her hair. "I thought you'd gone."

"Jacob." She clung to him, burying her face against his chest.

"I'm sorry." He leaned back, kissing her hard, tasting the saltiness of her tears. "I was an asshole. I didn't mean it, not any of it . . ."

"You were right," she hiccupped. "I didn't want it badly enough. I thought I was strong enough . . ."

"You are," he countered. "You are strong. You've made it this long . . ."

"By doing what?" She shoved away from him, knuckling tears off of her face. "You were right. I was just playing house, wasting time. I didn't want to face what I was afraid of." He watched as she swallowed convulsively, her face a mask of shame and pain. "I'm still a coward."

"No." He sighed. "You're not a coward."

"How would you know?" she asked scornfully. "And why are you even talking to me? I'm not *real*, remember? I'm just a figment of your subconscious . . . an unhelpful, useless illusion, at that!"

She turned, ready to head away from him, into the hotel. He looped his arms around her waist, holding tight when she struggled, swearing at him. "Please, please listen to me. I can't help the fact that it's hard for me to believe. Would you believe all this, if it were happening to you?"

"It *is* happening to me!" she spat out, jerking away from him. He followed her through the glass doors.

"If you were me," he persisted, "a doctor, and you started having sexual dreams about a patient, would you believe that it was someone in a coma actually talking to you while you slept?"

She slowed, and he stepped in front of her.

"You were cruel." Her eyes were like the moon, silvery and luminescent.

"I know. I'm sorry." He shook his head. "I didn't want to believe in you. I thought I was losing my mind."

"And now. . . ?"

He paused.

"You're still not convinced," she said. She rubbed her hands over her face.

"I'm close," he said. "And if you knew what I was like, before I met you, you would understand what a huge concession that is."

"I don't know you. For all I know, *I* invented *you*." She looked alarmed, then her face relaxed. "But I know that's not true. I know you're real."

For a second, he was fascinated by her certainty. "How can you be so sure?"

She shrugged. "I just am."

Her faith humbled him. Even though he'd always prided himself on being logical and rational, for a second, he envied her ability to simply believe, and go with her instinct.

"Where were you?" he asked, putting an arm around her shoulders. "I looked for you everywhere."

He could feel her shake, pressing tighter against his side. "I was taking your advice," she said with a trace of bitterness. "I was trying to wake up."

He stopped, startled. "You were? How?"

"I told you there were things on this island," she muttered. "Things that frightened me. Well, I went there."

"And. . . ?" He felt excitement—and, strangely, a little apprehension.

"I'm still here, aren't I?" she snapped. "It didn't work. I don't know how to get myself to wake up. But I don't ever want to go back there again."

"Back where?"

They headed toward her room, more out of habit than for any specific reason. "Back to the grove," she said. "When you head down the path, into the rain forest, there's a small village. Further on, there's a path that leads into the darkest part of the woods. That's where it happens."

"Where *what* happens?" Jacob pressed.

"Rituals." She shuddered. "I'm making myself a cup of tea."

He wanted to keep asking her, but she was obviously still

frightened, so he backed off, sitting on a barstool at the counter of her suite's kitchenette. He watched as she put the silver teakettle on to boil. "You've been there before?"

She nodded, her eyes looking haunted. "When I first arrived here, I had started to realize this wasn't just a dream— or if it was, it was the longest dream I'd ever been in," she said. "I decided to explore the island. Like you, I figured my subconscious was trying to 'tell' me something." She chuckled bitterly. "Every place seemed to be abandoned. Then I went to the woods. I heard music, drums, chanting. I figured it must be what I was looking for."

The teakettle whistled, and she started. Then she rummaged for a cup, pouring the boiling water over the teabag. Jacob waited patiently.

"There was a woman there," she said slowly, holding the teacup absently, warming her palms around it. "A tall, beautiful black woman. She had drawn something on the ground. There was an assortment of people around her. The chanting grew louder, and she started to dance."

Jacob found himself mesmerized. "Then what?"

"She fell to the ground, as if she were having a seizure," Rory said in horrified remembrance. "When she stood up, it seemed like her eyes had changed colors. There was a goat tethered, and she . . ." Rory gagged. "She slit its throat, catching the blood in a silver bowl."

Jacob's eyes widened.

"The crowd started to pass the bowl around," she said. "They started to sing. And drink." She put the teacup down with a clatter on the granite countertop. "That's when I noticed that they weren't really people. I don't know what they were, but they weren't human."

"And that's what frightened you?"

She stared at him. "It was more than that," she said. "If you saw them, *felt* them, you'd understand. The feelings were unbelievable. Overwhelming."

Jacob didn't understand. The answer seemed to lie there, in that grove. Granted, what she was describing sounded unpleasant, but at the same time, it was just a dream. Nothing could hurt her. "So, you went back there today?"

She nodded curtly. "I saw the same woman, the same . . . *people*."

"Did she kill anything else?"

Rory shook her head. "She was too busy having sex." She grimaced. "With two men."

Jacob choked at that one. "Why was she doing that?"

"Because one wasn't enough?" Rory said. "How should I know? She mentioned something about Erzuli."

"Erzuli . . ." Jacob frowned. "Wait. That sounds familiar. I think I remember my brother telling me something about that."

"She said that I couldn't leave," Rory continued. "She said that I'd leave when I die. She offered to teach me pleasure and power. Even offered to share her men with me."

Now Jacob was riveted. "What did you say?"

Rory paused, then smiled bitterly. "Why? Jealous?"

Jacob stood up, almost knocking the barstool over. "Yes."

Rory looked at him, surprised. "What if I'm not real?"

"I don't care." He closed the distance between them, kissing her hard. "Whatever you are, I don't want to lose you, Rory. I need you."

Her smile wasn't the bitter, ironic smile she'd been showing, the past few minutes. It was the smile he knew, pure and sweet and delighted. "I love you, Jacob," she breathed, kissing him back.

He froze. He'd never said the words. To anyone. She held him close, and he held her back, tight enough to bruise.

"I love you, too, Rory." Then he held her close to him.

She melted against him, and he cradled her, carrying her to the bed. They took turns removing each other's clothing, then stretched out next to each other, just holding each other. She pressed a tiny kiss on his shoulder. He caressed the curve of her hip, then stroked her back in long, lazy circles. They pressed together, warmth seeping between them as their flesh met and melded. He kissed her slowly, and she hooked her leg over his hip, curling around him. He positioned his cock and entered her, slowly, lovingly. They moved like dancers listening to their own private, slow love ballad. He entered and retreated, each movement a litany to how he felt about her. It was gentle and tender and endless.

When they finally climaxed together, shuddering against each other with quiet, breathless gasps, he kissed her again. *I love you*, he thought. *No matter what, I love you.*

She fell asleep, obviously wrung out by both their argument and the day's events. She was curled up protectively. He covered her with a light blanket, stroking her cheek. She didn't stir.

He got up, got dressed quietly, and left the room.

Go down the path, he told himself, hurrying. *Past the village, into the heart of the forest . . .*

He loved her, whether she was real or not. But he still had to find out if she really was real.

He made it past the poor village and headed toward the dark interior of the rain forest. Just as she'd described, he heard chanting and the rising sound of music and drumming. He walked toward the sounds.

When he entered the clearing, he saw the strange figures she had spoken of. They looked like humans, but there was something strange about them. A feeling of foreboding chilled him to his bones. He ignored it.

It's just a dream, he told himself sternly.

Of course, if Rory *was* real, then what was this?

The drumming stopped. A tall man wearing a black hat and suit stared at him. "What are you doing here? How dare you interrupt our ritual?"

Jacob suddenly fell to his knees. His heart seemed to stop in his chest, and he found himself gasping for air.

"Baron Samedi, please," a woman's voice purred, and the pressure suddenly abated. Jacob clutched at his chest, taking gulping breaths. He looked up.

A stunning woman, dressed in a scarlet sarong, was standing in front of him. She was beautiful, but there was an aura of danger around her. "Naughty boy," she said, her voice husky. She stroked his face. "What brings you to my island? I didn't invite you here—but now that I've seen you, I can't say that I mind one bit."

His cock went hard in a flash, embarrassing him. She

simply laughed, continuing to touch him. When he finally backed away, her eyes flashed—in surprise, he assumed. And anger.

"You're not one of mine," she announced, and there was a grumble among the things assembled. "What brings you here?"

"What did you tell Rory?"

"Rory?" She stared. "That . . . that *child* called you here? To *my* realm?"

"Who are you?" he gasped. "*What* are you?"

"I am Serafina," she replied, her back straightening, her breasts jutting out proudly. "I am the most powerful vodun priestess to ever live."

And with those words, Jacob felt a pull, something stronger than he'd ever felt. As she stared at him, he suddenly had the urge to walk to her, to press his mouth on her breasts and her sex, to do whatever she told him to do . . .

Rory.

Like a small voice of sanity, he pictured Rory's face, heard her in his mind. Hanging on to that, he gritted his teeth, staying where he stood.

"Impressive," Serafina said derisively. "She's got more power than I thought, to involve an outsider."

"You're a dream," he said. "This is all a dream."

She shrugged. "So?"

"So you can't really hurt me," he said. "Tell me: how can Rory leave this dream? How can she wake up?"

"I'll tell you what I told the girl," Serafina replied. "She can't wake. The only way she can leave is by dying."

"How did she get here?" Jacob demanded. "Why is she trapped in this place?"

"Do you really want to know?" Serafina walked past him, and he could feel her perfume brushing past him like the whisper of silk. "Look, and I'll show you."

She pointed to the ground. There was a drawing, a symbol, formed of some kind of powder. The lines suddenly started to shift and move, like liquid, forming a picture, clear as any television.

He watched in fascination as a younger Mr. and Mrs. Jacquard stood in the same clearing, with Serafina looking the same age, just as dangerously beautiful. Mr. Jacquard scowled, but Mrs. Jacquard's face showed a heartbreaking desperation.

"Can you help us, Serafina?" Mrs. Jacquard said, in her exquisitely cultured voice.

"I can," Serafina answered. "For a price."

"Of course," Mr. Jacquard scoffed.

"Not money, Henri," Serafina said with a smile. "The residents of this island know how powerful I am. They come to me because they trust me to help them. I am their leader. But my power needs a wider audience."

She strode around them, like a cat circling prey. "I will help you have a baby," she said. "When she is born, you will have a party, inviting your rich off-island society friends. And there, you will introduce me as the reason you were finally able to conceive. You will recognize me, in front of everyone, and tell them of my power and how I helped you. Is that clear?"

"This is ludicrous," Mr. Jacquard said, starting to walk away. But Mrs. Jacquard held his arm.

"Henri," she pleaded. "We've tried everything else."

He looked into her eyes. Then he kissed her, his expression more loving and tender than Jacob would have ever thought possible. Mr. Jacquard turned to Serafina. "All right. We agree to your price."

In the picture, Serafina's smile was cruelly triumphant.

The picture shifted, changed, then vanished. "They knew the price," Serafina said, as the picture disappeared. "They broke it. So I cursed the child, as I told them I would."

"Rory's here because of a voodoo curse?"

"Don't sound so skeptical," Serafina shot back. "You are also here because of voodoo. The fact that you could enter this realm without my knowledge suggests you have some power. But hear me now: if I decide you're too much of a bother, I will hurt you. Or worse. Stay away from Rory."

The overwhelming unreality of the moment struck Jacob like a hammer. "You're a *dream*! Just a dream!"

"Am I?"

With that, she reached out, clawing his chest with her nails. He hissed at the slicing pain. Then she pulled back, her fingernails red with his blood.

"Remember me, *doctor*," she said.

Jacob sat up in bed, abruptly awake. He reached down. His shirt stuck to his chest. There were red streaks. When he peeled the material away, there were four horizontal nail marks, dragged down his chest.

*   *   *

"Jacob, I'm really starting to worry about you," Aaron said, watching his brother warily.

Jacob paced through Aaron's apartment as if he'd drunk fourteen cups of coffee. He moved frantically, with almost a slight tremble, and his eyes were wild. If Aaron didn't know how tightly controlled his brother was, he would've suspected that Jacob had indulged in some kind of drug or something to get him so wired. Jacob finally looked at Aaron with wild, bright eyes.

"She's real," Jacob said firmly. "Rory's real, and she's been communicating with me, I swear to God. It's not a hallucination."

Aaron sighed. This was what was causing him the most concern. "Just like I told you on the phone, Jacob—she couldn't possibly be."

"Listen, I know you think I'm crazy." Jacob stopped walking, but he tapped his hand against his leg, obviously without thought. "I've wondered myself. But there's just too much that points to this being real."

"Like what?"

"The damned raccoon—the one she rescued when she was five," Jacob pointed out. "I even knew its name. How could I have possibly known about that? No one in her family told me before she did; it wasn't in any of the case files. How could I have known about that?"

Aaron shifted uncomfortably in his chair. "Coincidence," he tried, but knew it was unconvincing.

"And her brain wave activity," Jacob pressed. "All the doctors prior to me failed to create any change in her mental state. Now, with these dreams, she's showing improvement. And she only has activity when I'm asleep. When I'm *with* her."

"You still have no proof that there's a correlation."

"She's *real*, goddammit!" Jacob roared.

Aaron stayed silent, his body tensed. The brother he knew would never get involved in a fistfight. But right now, Jacob wasn't the brother he knew, and he looked ready to take a swing at someone, and Aaron was handy. "I'm just playing devil's advocate," he said, keeping his voice mild even as he got out of his chair, fists beginning to ball.

Jacob glared at him . . . then took a deep breath, collapsing into the couch. He rubbed at his chest, obviously unconsciously. "I'm sorry," he muttered. "I'm not making my case well, acting like this. You must think I'm a lunatic."

Aaron wasn't sure if this was real or a ruse, so he stayed standing. "So what do you want me to do?"

"I want you to help me."

Aaron felt a little twinge of relief. "Okay. I don't think we want to do anything as radical as antipsychotics, but I can prescribe—"

"No." Jacob's voice cut across harshly. "I want you to help me with Rory."

Now Aaron frowned. "With your patient? How? That's not my field."

"I think I know what did this to her." Jacob paused, his mouth puckering as if he'd eaten a sour cherry. "If you didn't believe me before, this certainly isn't going to help matters, but . . . I think she's been cursed."

"Cursed." Aaron drew out the word.

Maybe I should have him put away for a seventy-two-hour psychiatric evaluation. He eyed the phone, calculating whom he should call and how he would restrain Jacob.

Jacob stood, obviously sensing Aaron's intent. "Hear me out first, okay?" When Aaron nodded, he continued. "In the dream, she took me to see a dark part of the island, where they held rituals. There was a priestess. A voodoo priestess."

At the word *voodoo*, Aaron felt enveloped in ice.

"Apparently, Rory's parents went to this woman because they couldn't conceive. She promised to help them, in return for introducing her to their rich off-island friends. If they didn't follow through with their end of the bargain, Rory would be cursed to live as less than a zombie from the first moment she tried to lose her viginity."

"Are you kidding me?" Aaron blurted out.

"Do I fucking look like I'm kidding you?" Jacob snapped back. "I *know* how it sounds. But that's what I saw, what I experienced. And I need to figure out if this is true or not."

Aaron felt dread start to rise in his stomach. "What do you need me to do?"

Jacob's expression was set. "That woman, the one you were seeing . . ."

Aaron closed his eyes. "Mahjani." Even saying her name was uncomfortable.

"She's a professor of that kind of thing, isn't she? Over at NYU?"

"Comparative theology, with an emphasis on tribal magic and lore, yes." Aaron sounded defensive. How often had he defended Mahjani's background to a member of his family, or his elite intellectual friends, by using the overblown job definition?

Worse, how often had he failed to defend her?

"I want you to talk to her," Jacob said. "I need you to find out if she would be willing to help, somehow. If she even thinks she can help."

"Why don't I just give you her phone number?"

Jacob looked at him, askance, and Aaron felt like a coward. Probably because that was exactly what he was being. "After the way you left things," Jacob said bluntly, "I doubt that saying I'm your brother is going to get her to listen to me."

Aaron winced.

"Listen, if I had time to research this, I would, but you've got a ready connection, and I'm sorry, but I really need you to move past whatever happened with this woman and help me out." Jacob's eyes blazed with desperation. "Please, Aaron. I really, really need your help. Just smooth things over with the woman, let her know how important this is, and get her to talk to me, okay? Please?"

It must have cost him tremendously, to beg like this.

"I'll call her," Aaron promised, with a sigh. "I can't guarantee anything, but . . ."

"Thank you." Jacob stood immediately, the manic frenzy back on him. "I have to get back. When you get her help, could you call me? Any time, day or night."

"Listen, I told you, she might not cooperate." Aaron felt like he was being barreled along on a freight train.

"You'll think of something." Jacob smiled, a ghost of his

normal, reserved grin. It held a twinge of bitterness. "You're the charming one in the family, after all. The emotional one."

"Yeah, yeah. Whatever." Aaron's response was quick and reflexive, since it was a perennial jab: Aaron, the psychiatrist, the only "emotional" one in a family of rational, scientific medical geniuses.

Jacob paused in the open doorway of Aaron's apartment. "I owe you," he said quietly. "You need anything—want anything I have—it's yours."

That took Aaron aback, and he laughed nervously. "Well, I've always had an eye on that Lexus of yours . . ."

Jacob dug into his pocket, holding out the key.

"I was kidding," Aaron said, shaken. "Does this case really mean that much to you, then?"

"She means everything to me."

The vehement way that Jacob made the statement only made Aaron more worried. But at the same time, he saw a passion . . . a *life* that his reserved brother had never shown before. He was making a sort of breakthrough.

He might also be having a psychotic episode, the professional part of Aaron's brain commented caustically.

Right now, Aaron wasn't acting as a doctor, though. He was acting as a brother.

After Jacob left, Aaron poured himself a large glass of scotch, taking a few manful sips of the stuff. Like the rest of his family, he was too enamored with control to indulge overly in any kind of mind-altering substance, but the prospect of facing Mahjani, even over the phone, was something that needed a little liquid courage.

He dialed her number from memory—even after a year, his fingers still traced the familiar pattern easily. He realized his heart rate had accelerated, and he swallowed nervously as he listened to the phone ring.

After the fourth ring, he realized that she probably wasn't going to pick up—that he was going to get an answering machine. He felt a combination of regret and relief, trying to mentally prepare the message he was going to leave: *Mahjani, this is Aaron White. I need to talk to you. Could you please—*

"Hello?"

Caught off guard, Aaron cleared his throat. "Mahjani?"

There was a long pause. "Aaron." There was no questioning in her voice.

"You don't sound surprised," Aaron noted inanely.

"I'm not."

She didn't elaborate. Considering how long it had been since he'd so unceremoniously dumped her, he wondered why she was expecting to hear from him.

Probably something creepy and "hoodoo" and superstitious told her that you were going to call.

"Still the same old Aaron," she added. "What do you want?"

He had the disquieting feeling that she had read his mind, and he immediately felt guilty—and irritated. "I need your help."

"My help?" Now she did sound surprised. "With what?"

"With . . . your background. I need someone who's an expert in your field. I need you." The minute he said the words, he flinched.

I need you.

How often had he said that . . . usually when they were entwined, naked, writhing in his bed?

"You can't even say it," she scoffed. "Why in the world would you need help with voodoo, Aaron? Got an enemy who's giving you trouble? Need to win some pretty, *suitable* woman's heart?"

The bitterness dripped from her words like acid.

"My brother is working with a coma patient. He thinks she's been cursed. He needs to speak to you." The words came out clipped, hard as diamonds. "If you want to help, fine. Otherwise, I'll find someone else."

Another long pause. Then a sigh.

"I see. Fine, then."

He felt a little victory . . . until her next statement.

"Find someone else."

The click was followed by the long blare of the dial tone.

"Shit." He dialed back. The phone kept ringing . . . she'd obviously unplugged it.

He found himself getting up, putting on his coat. He'd mishandled this, as he'd mishandled so many other things. But his brother, the emotionally closed, super neurologist, needed help from his kid brother, the "touchy-feely" shrink. If he could get through to Mahjani, he might have a solution to his brother's problem—and potentially help him stop Jacob's imminent breakdown.

He walked out the door at a fast clip.

If Aaron knew Mahjani's number by heart, he also knew it took exactly thirty minutes to get to her apartment.

Chapter Six

Mahjani Rafallo sat in her apartment in Brooklyn, sipping a cup of kava tea, trying to steady her nerves. She had known that Aaron was going to call: the loas, her spirits, had told her that he was going to reenter her life. But she hadn't known how or why. To have him call was startling. To have him ask for help was mind-blowing.

To have him issue an ultimatum in that cold, clinical voice was more than she could stand.

There was a banging knock on her door. She jumped, spilling some of the hot tea on her hand. Hissing in pain, she put the cup down, looking out the fish-eye lens of her peephole.

"Mahjani, open up. It's Aaron."

Her heart clenched in her chest. "Go away." To her relief, her voice barely shook.

"I have to talk to you."

"We don't have anything to say to each other."

"Listen, this is important." His voice was harsh. "I'm sorry, okay? I shouldn't have been such a prick on the phone, but this is urgent."

She crossed her arms. "Just go away!" Now she sounded more emotional, less controlled. It couldn't be helped.

She could hear him sigh heavily from the other side of the door. "My brother's in trouble," he said, and the edge of worry in his voice was palpable. "I think you can help him. Please. Please talk to me."

She felt her icy reserve start to melt. His brother was the only one in Aaron's family who gave a shit about him: the two were close, closer than even they liked to admit. If there was anyone who Aaron would walk over fire for, it would be Jacob.

She bit her lower lip, then slowly unlocked the deadbolt and slid the chain off its latch. "You have five minutes." She gestured him inside curtly.

"Thank you."

As he walked past her, she caught a whiff of his scent: something subtle and expensive, mixed with the masculinity that was all him . . . sort of woodsy and natural. She shivered slightly. He'd cut his hair, she noticed. It was shorter than it had been a year ago. Otherwise, he looked just as handsome and mouthwatering as he had looked when she'd met him at that party in Manhattan: looking too rich, too upper-crust and too out of her league to mess with.

Her fingers itched to touch him. She stuffed her hands in her pockets.

"What's wrong with Jacob?" she asked.

Aaron looked stiff, stubborn. "He has a patient that's been in a coma for six years. He thinks she's been put under a voodoo curse."

"A voodoo curse?" Mahjani's eyes widened. "*Your* brother?"

"I know." Aaron laughed facetiously. "This case has him crazed. He's not himself."

"He wouldn't be, if he honestly believes that." Mahjani crossed her arms, trying to get into the mindset of the vodun priestess she was. Pretend that Aaron wasn't her ex-lover but was just here to get her help and healing. "Does he know who cursed her, then? Or what the effects are supposed to be?"

Aaron looked surprised. He leaned against a wall. "I'm sorry. I guess I wasn't clear."

Mahjani felt her stomach drop. He sounded embarrassed. For her. "I thought you needed my help," she remarked carefully.

"I do." Aaron's face set. "I need your help to convince Jacob that what he's suggesting isn't possible."

Her mouth fell open.

"My brother's in a terribly confused state right now." Aaron's voice was low, rich . . . persuasive. "I think he's on the edge of a mental breakdown. The last thing I want to do is keep playing along with this charade. You are an expert on voodoo practices. You can show him that what he's doing is simply deluding himself, reaching for straws because he can't cure this girl."

Mahjani felt nauseous. It was just like when he broke up with her, all over again.

We're from two different worlds, Mahjani. I love you—but it just can't work.

He didn't believe in what she believed in. He belittled it in so many subtle and blatant ways. In turn, he condescended to her, and her life.

"What if he's not deluding himself?" She took a step closer to Aaron, her hands balled in fists at her sides. "What if the girl really is cursed?"

"Mahjani, this isn't some superstitious, psychosomatic, easily influenced kid from the islands," he said, and each word was like a razor, slashing at her heart. "This is a wealthy girl from the Hamptons, for Christ's sake. And she's in a medically documented coma, and has been for six years. Who puts *themselves* in a coma for six years?"

"You don't know the toxins that people are exposed to in voodoo," she argued. "And you don't know anything about the rituals. It moves beyond superstition."

He reached forward, gripping her upper arms painfully. "Damn it, Mahjani, I'm not playing with you here!" He gave her a little shake. "This is my brother's sanity I'm talking about. I'm not going to encourage him right over the fucking edge because you want to convince me that your 'faith' is valid!"

She put her hands flat on his chest, shoving him against the wall, even as he still clutched her. "I'm not playing," she growled back. "You're so blind that you refuse to see that I might be the only person to help your brother, *and* this girl. You'd rather let him go insane facing something he knows nothing about, than admit there might be a possibility

beyond what your science-worshiping bastard parents believe in!"

The words were like daggers, lying between them. They
were both breathing heavily, close to each other, anger making
the air electric. She stared into his warm hazel eyes, flashing
with temper and passion and concern . . . and yearning.

She knew all about yearning.

It would only be an inch or two to lean forward and taste
that mouth of his, feel the firmness of his lips against hers. It
would only take the smallest of movements to press her body
against his. She could feel the heat coming off him, through
the thick layers of his camel-hair coat and tailored suit. She
ached to feel him, bare and vulnerable inside her.

She closed her eyes and then took a crucial step back.

To her surprise, Aaron followed her, stepping forward,
pulling her to him. Before she could stop him, his mouth was
on her, just as she'd wanted it. His kiss was forceful, almost
punishing in its intensity. She met him, her hands bunching
in the luxurious fabric of his coat as his tongue swept past her
lips, penetrating her mouth. She gasped against him, clinging to him.

He tilted his face, his mouth devouring hers. She could
feel passion humming through him like a tuning fork. When
he finally pulled away from her, he took a strangled breath.
"Jesus," he blurted out. "I shouldn't have done that."

Still, he didn't release her.

Her body sang with pent-up desire. "I've missed you," she
admitted in a ragged voice. "There hasn't been anyone since
you."

It took so much for her to make that concession. Her soul felt naked.

He crushed her to him, stroking her hair, her back. "Mah-jani." The word was torn from him. "I've never stopped thinking about you."

She leaned her head against his chest, tears stinging at her eyes. She'd wanted to hear that, and now that she had, it was a slight balm. "Can't we start over?" she murmured. "Can't we . . . fix this, somehow?"

He stroked his hands down her arms, then gently nudged her a step back. His woebegone eyes told her before his voice did, and her heart sank.

"I don't see how." He sounded apologetic—and defensive.

It shouldn't have hurt more than the first time. Instead, it was worse. The first time he'd rejected her was like a knife cut, sharp and quick. This was like a burn, slow and growing in intensity. She thought she'd healed from the first time.

Now she didn't know how long it would take to recover.

He sighed. "When I started seeing you, I knew how much I wanted you. But when it came to a relationship—I thought that we would be more compatible. I thought because you were a professor at NYU it meant that you were more . . ." He gestured futilely, trying to come up with the word.

"You thought I was more logical," she responded numbly. "More scientific."

"Yes." His eyes pleaded for understanding. It made the hurt worse. "Then, when I found out you . . . well, that you actually put some credence in these things . . ."

"You found out I practiced what I taught." She figured that would be it.

"First, I figured it wouldn't have anything to do with us," he said. "Then, I thought as long as no one else knew about it . . ."

"You were ashamed of me." There was no venom in her voice, only a tired anger. She'd had a year to process this. Fury had died into a bitter sort of regret. "I know."

At least he looked embarrassed. "I just don't buy into all this."

"You don't believe in anything you can't see and touch."

He nodded. "Exactly."

"Including love."

"That's not fair," he said, but she felt like she was on the edge of crying. She wasn't going to do that to herself. He'd seen enough of her tears.

"It was stupid of me to ask," she said, walking across her living room and drinking from her cup of tea, struggling for control. "Just leave me your brother's number. I'll handle it from there."

When she turned, he was staring at her warily. "You'd call my brother?"

She nodded.

"And tell him what?"

"I need to find out more about his situation if I'm going to help him," she said, shifting into the role of voodoo priestess once more. "Even if you don't believe in what I can do, I do have a lot of experience. If she's really cursed, and Jacob wants to cure her, then he might be in danger himself. I would—"

"No. I don't want you talking to him." Aaron's eyes were cold. "Not about that. I don't want him retreating further into this delusion."

It's not delusion, you ass! She grimaced. "Why don't you let me be the judge of that?"

But she could tell on his face that he didn't trust her. The pain roiled through her.

"Your brother could be in more danger than you know," she argued. "Would you really subject him to that, simply because of your prejudices?"

"I'm trying to keep him safe." His voice was like a whip, quick and cutting.

"So am I," she said.

He took a deep breath, then shook his head. "I'm sorry I came here."

She closed her eyes. A solitary tear leaked out. "I'm sorry you came here, too."

She heard his footsteps, soft and quick across her thick carpet. Then the door opened, and closed.

He was gone without a word.

She threw the cup across the room, letting it shatter, the tea dripping down her wall. Then she sank onto her floor and wept.

Rory woke alone in her bed, shivering slightly. She thought it was evening, but no, it was simply overcast. A storm was hitting the island. In the entire time she'd been on the island, she couldn't remember it ever drizzling, much less seeing anything like the dark, ponderous thunderclouds that were threatening on the horizon.

She sat up, feeling wrung out.

Jacob must be awake now, she thought, stretching. She wondered what he was doing. What he was thinking? She got up, forcing herself to get dressed. She wasn't . . .

She stopped.

There were sounds.

She crept to the doorway of her hotel room, pressing her ear against the wood of the door.

People. Down the hallway, she could hear people laughing, walking around.

She got dressed quickly, her heart beating frantically. Had the creatures from the grove invaded her sanctuary? Were they getting even with her for interrupting their rituals by switching over to the only place she felt safe?

Wearing a pair of jeans, a tank top, and a pair of sneakers, she crept out into the hallway. The noise intensified: it sounded more and more like the thrum of a crowd, the busy, shuffling sounds of people walking to and fro. It sounded like a busy hotel, she thought.

A well-dressed couple walked past her without even looking at her, engrossed in their own conversation. "Can't believe Henri and Lily bought this place," one said.

Rory started. *Henri and Lily.*

Those were her parents' names. It couldn't be coincidence.

She followed the couple, merging into a stream of other obviously rich people who were populating the hotel. The place was now swarmed with well-to-do tourists. The reception desk was packed with people. To help them put up with the indignity of waiting in line, a young woman handed out crystal flutes full of mimosas from a silver tray. Porters dashed around like ants, pushing heavy carts filled with matching, monogrammed luggage. Above the great glass doors was a huge sign: CONGRATULATIONS, HENRI AND LILY!

"Congratulations for what?" Rory mumbled.

"Their baby," a woman said, looking over Rory's casual garb with distaste. "I take it you're not here for the christening party, then."

Rory shook her head. Christening party. If it were her parents, they only had one child—her. So the party would be . . . for her? As a baby?

Why am I dreaming this?

She was jostled by the crowd, following them mindlessly as they streamed toward the tall-ceilinged ballroom. The people were crushed in there, celebrating with champagne and caviar and tiny pastries. In the midst of the commotion, there was a loud, ceremonious *gong,* and a man stood up at the top of the balustrade, over the ballroom's orchestra pit.

Rory looked up . . . and almost fainted.

It was her father, not as she had last seen him, but as he had been years ago. She remembered pictures. He had to be thirty-four at the oldest. He was smiling broadly. She couldn't remember the last time she had seen him so happy. He hugged her mother to his side in open affection. Rory was astounded, and touched.

Her father waved his hands. "Thank you all for coming, and for being patient while checking in." There were a number of chuckles at that, as well as some good-natured grumbling. "This hotel has been a dream of mine for years. Then I met Lily, and I thought I couldn't be happier. Well, I was wrong."

Her mother was stunning, wearing a pale peach wrap dress, her hair up in a loose blond chignon. She reached into a stroller behind her, producing a swaddled baby. A tiny pink arm emerged from the folds of blanket, and a lusty baby cry followed.

"Now, I can honestly say that I couldn't be happier!"

There were loud cheers. The pride and love in her father's voice was so clear, Rory felt tears misting her eyes. She missed them, she realized. They were overprotective, yes. She had her differences with them, about everything, it seemed. But they loved her so much. It had been so long since she'd seen them. Too long.

If I don't wake up, then I'll never see them again.

It was a truth she hadn't wanted to contemplate. Now, seeing this snapshot of their happy history, she felt an overwhelming sadness.

"Please, enjoy yourselves . . ."

"Wait!"

The loud shout sounded like thunder, and everyone in the ballroom fell silent. Rory felt a chill of dread seep into her chest.

Serafina strode across the ballroom, the crowd parting like the Red Sea before her. She walked up the steps slowly.

"I think you forgot to invite someone," she said, and though she didn't raise her voice, it still echoed and boomed through the ballroom. There was a ripple of whispering through the assembled crowd.

Her mother took the baby—the younger Rory—and hid behind her father. Rory watched in horror as Serafina approached them.

"Did you forget my price so quickly?" She looked calm, even though her tone was caustic. "It's only been ten months, after all."

More whispers.

"You don't belong here," Rory's father said, his face turning pale with anger. "Get out." He gestured to some burly security guards. They started to move in on Serafina, but one glance from her had them freezing in their tracks.

"You were supposed to introduce me to these fine people," Serafina purred. "You were supposed to help me spread my reputation beyond this tiny island."

"You're a local nutcase," Rory's father said, and even Rory winced. "You didn't do anything, we don't owe you anything. *We have no agreement.*"

With that, Rory felt a strangling sensation, and she was immediately light-headed.

This. This is why I'm here.

She fought her way to the exit, ignoring the curious murmurs and comments of the crowd, who were aghast.

"You will pay for my services," was the last thing she heard Serafina say. "One way or another."

Rory forced her way out of the hotel, onto the grass lawn. She hugged her stomach, struggling not to retch.

What she had just seen had happened years ago. She was obviously far too young to remember, and her parents had never shared this story with her, but she knew that it was true.

Locals from the village were coming up the path. They ignored her, as well, heading with grim determination toward the resort.

"No," Rory said, as she saw their lit torches, the wine bottles with rags stuffed in the necks. "No! Please, stop!"

But it was too late.

The hotel caught slowly, but once the fire took, it spread with increasing speed. Screaming tourists fled the building. Rory watched as her parents, cradling her, ran with the rest of the crowd toward the beaches, the docks. By nightfall, the hotel was a smoldering pile of ash and coals.

Serafina was the last to leave. She walked up to Rory.

"You see what I'm capable of," she whispered, her eyes unnaturally bright, glowing. "You don't want to cross me. You tell that to that man of yours, as well."

"That man . . ." Rory started to echo, then abruptly shut her mouth.

Jacob.

"He came to see me," Serafina said with a wink. "He thinks he's stronger. Men always do. But I'll hurt him if he comes back. You're mine, and you're here, Rory. Best get used to it." She pointed to the hotel. "Next time, I won't just take your pretty little bedroom."

With that, Serafina headed back to the grove, leaving Rory to stare . . . and think.

Chapter Seven

"No, Jacob. I've let this go too far as it is," Aaron said over the phone. "If you're not going to do something about this delusion of yours, then I'm going to."

Jacob rubbed at his temple with one hand while holding the cell phone to his ear with the other. "Listen, I shouldn't have gotten you involved. If you just give me her phone number, I'll take it from there." He didn't know what the history was between Aaron and the woman, but he knew that it ended poorly—and that Aaron, despite dating plenty of eligible women, really mourned the loss of that particular relationship, despite his being the one who pulled the trigger on it.

"I don't want you talking to her, or anyone else," Aaron snapped. "This is crazy. Do you understand that?"

"Spoken like a shrink."

"You're not going to distract me with that petty sibling rivalry bullshit." Aaron sounded livid. "You're a doctor, goddammit. You have a responsibility to your patient."

That stung. "Believe me, no one is more on my mind."

"Yeah. You're thinking about screwing her," Aaron pointed out. "She's in a coma, Jacob. Jesus! Do you know what that makes you?"

Jacob's stomach turned with a nauseating twist. "I haven't touched her physical body, beyond examination. My protocols have been impeccable."

"But you're becoming obsessed with her, nonetheless."

Angry as he was, Jacob knew his brother was right. Unfortunately, that wasn't going to stop him. "She needs me, Aaron. If you're not going to help me, so be it. But I know I'm right this time, and I'm going to do whatever I have to to wake Rory up."

"You're risking your professional career. You're risking everything that's ever meant anything in your life, and all you can say is you know you're right?" Aaron was just short of yelling. "Are you really that egotistical?"

"I love her, Aaron."

Aaron fell silent on the other end of the line, and Jacob knew he'd finally admitted too much. Bad enough that he was thinking in sexual terms with a patient—even if all he'd ever done was in dreams. But to have fallen in love with someone he was treating?

Jacob sighed heavily. "I know how bad it looks, Aaron."

"I should report you," Aaron said. "This isn't like you, at all. This is dangerous."

"Just give me a little time—"

"You're losing your mind, Jake."

"Just two weeks," Jacob pleaded. "If nothing happens in the next two weeks that might convince you, then I'll back off. You can have me examined; I'll go to counseling . . ."

"You'll take yourself off this case."

Jacob winced. Go away from Rory?

Like hell.

"We'll see," he conceded.

"No," Aaron replied. "I'll give you two weeks. If there's no improvement—if she's not *awake*—then you quit this case and go away from this family. Otherwise, I'll call the medical board now, and strongly suggest that they compel you to have a psychiatric examination."

"You're supposed to be my brother," Jacob growled. "You're supposed to help me!"

Now it was Aaron's turn to sigh. "I am your brother. And believe it or not, I care about you," he said, which was as close to saying *love* as their family ever got. "Which is why I'm trying to save you from yourself."

"Fine." Jacob clicked off the phone, then shut off the light, burrowing deeper under the covers.

Two weeks. It wasn't a lot of time—especially when he still had no idea how to wake Rory up.

He fell asleep, quickly and easily, just like he always did now. Like clockwork, he awoke on the island—only this time, he did not arrive in the luxurious suite he was used to. He was on the grounds.

Rather, he was on what was left of the grounds.

The exposed, charred beams of the hotel were still smoking. The air reeked of burning wood and ash.

Fear spiked through him. "Rory?" he called, looking around frantically. "Rory!"

"I'm here," he heard her voice call from the nearby beach.

He sprinted to her, wrapping his arms around her. "What happened to the hotel?"

"Serafina burned it down," she said. "I think that they burned it down in real life, when I was a baby. My parents used to own this hotel. I was born on this island."

He processed that, even as he tried as best he could to comfort her. She was now without shelter. He knew that Serafina was trying to strip Rory down emotionally, cause her to crack. To what purpose, though? "So Serafina told you about your parents? About the deal they made?"

She pulled away, staring at him in surprised horror. "You knew?"

He winced. "I spoke with Serafina, when you were sleeping. I thought I could find a way to wake you . . ."

"That's why," Rory said. "That's why she burned the place down. She didn't know you could come here until I mentioned your name. When you showed up . . ." Rory shivered, rubbing her hands along her arms as if she were freezing. "She's angry that you're here, and she's angry that I'm trying to wake up. She's going to do something to me if I don't get out of here soon. I can feel it."

Jacob thought back to his conversation with Serafina.

I will hurt you. Or worse.

He believed she was capable of hurting him. At this point, though, he wasn't worried about himself. He was worried about Rory.

Nothing could hurt him more than something happening to her.

"We've got to get you out of here. We've got to get you to wake up, somehow."

Rory nodded, looking determined. "I know. The problem is how?"

"I'm not sure," he muttered, holding her and looking around at the devastation. This was all happening too fast. He had a two-week deadline, before his brother reported him to the medical board or tried to have him psychiatrically evaluated. Now, Rory was homeless and at the mercy of an egomaniacal voodoo priestess intent on either winning her over or possibly killing her. He had to wake her up—but he was just a doctor, not a witch doctor.

How the hell do you undo a curse?

"When I wake up, I'm doing a hell of a lot of Google searching," he muttered.

"Do you really think that will help?" she said, looking bewildered.

He realized—she'd been asleep for six years. Long enough to know what Google was, but not enough to realize what the Internet had turned into. "It'll turn up something. And there's a professor in New York that might be able to help us, if I can just get her to listen. If push comes to shove, there are other voodoo practitioners in New York, I'm sure. One of them will be able to help."

She nodded. "I'll do whatever you need me to do," she promised.

"First things first, then," he said, rolling up his sleeves. "We've got to get you some kind of shelter. Come on."

They explored the nearby rain forest, searching for something that wasn't too far from the wreckage of the hotel. After an hour of searching, they found a cave, near a clearing of sorts. It wasn't much, but it would shelter her from the elements, give her a place to hide.

"Hopefully you won't have to stay here long."

She nodded, looking determined. "No. I won't stay here long."

They went back to the hotel, scavenging. By nightfall, they had outfitted the cave with a few lanterns, a low table, and a mound of salvaged bedding.

"It's like a nest," she said reflectively.

The lanterns were lit. The place was very primitive, compared to the opulent splendor of the hotel.

He looked over at her. Her face was smudged with ash, her gold hair tangled. Her clothes were dirty, torn.

She looked beautiful.

He stroked her face, then held her close to him. He kissed her, and she kissed him back, no inhibitions, just pure, simple ardor.

"I'm so lucky I found you," he murmured against her throat, sucking gently.

"I'm the lucky one," she responded, rubbing her pelvis against his. "I feel like I've waited my whole life for you."

"I'll get you out of this, I swear."

"I know." Her eyes shone with trust. "I believe you, Jacob."

He felt like he was ten feet tall. After a lifetime of proving himself, he was intoxicated with the one person who simply believed in him, no questions asked.

He lifted her up, placing her gently in the center of their makeshift "bed." He burrowed into the bedding with her. They shed their clothes, reaching for each other. For a long time, they simply held each other, kissing each other slowly, their tongues caressing each other's as their bodies rubbed one over the other. Her thigh stroked against his; his hand rubbed her hip as it curved into her stomach; her palm stroked his back with warm, strong circles. It wasn't foreplay, although it was arousing them both. It was just happiness at being close to each other, reveling in each other's warmth and presence.

"Rory," he breathed. "I want to be with you forever."

"You will be." She kissed him fervently. "You will be."

With that, he entered her, his cock pressing into her pussy with a slow caress. They moved with exquisite delicacy, their lovemaking a ballet of sensuality. She nudged him over, straddling him, moving up and down his cock by inches, then resting astride him, his cock buried deep in her cunt. She arched her back and he felt her shift and clutch around him, causing him to moan with pleasure as she made tiny movements with her hips. She leaned almost all the way back, with yoga-styled flexibility, and he felt his cock stretching, plunging deep within her.

He sat up, pulling her hips against his, then leaned back.

Like a seesaw, the two of them took turns, one pressing and thrusting, the other relaxing and releasing. The climax built with infinitesimal slowness, but by the time the climax was on them they had created a conflagration that was unbelievable. They both sat, facing each other, their legs crossed, her thighs around his hips. They pressed against each other, sighing and gasping every time his cock was fully buried inside her.

"Jacob," she breathed, her head thrown back, her eyes closed.

He felt her pussy clench around him, and he gave up, pouring himself inside her, the orgasm shuddering through him for what felt like hours. When he was finished, they both rolled onto the bed, still holding each other tight.

I love you, he thought, kissing her passionately. Then he fell asleep, still buried inside her snug pussy, still holding her as if he never wanted to let her go.

When he woke, he was in his own bed, by himself. He had never felt so brutally alone.

I'm going to have to turn him in.

Aaron tossed and turned beneath his covers, then glanced at the ruby glow of his digital clock: 2:00 a.m.

Jacob had always been a hero of sorts for Aaron. The thought of reporting him to the medical board for inappropriate behavior was abhorrent. Still, Jacob was talking about voodoo . . . and sexual fantasies, and believing in telepathy.

What am I supposed to do? Let him actually buy into all this madness?

He let out an angry growl, then flung himself on his back.

What if Jacob's license was stripped? The shame would be unbearable. His life would be ruined. It wasn't like Jacob had anything besides his work. Not that Aaron could really throw stones at that assessment anymore: since he'd broken up with Mahjani, he'd gotten more and more engrossed in work, as well.

Mahjani. Another reason for his sleeplessness.

Aaron scrunched his eyes shut. He had been right. Mahjani would not have helped the situation. She would have exacerbated it. And how would it have looked to his parents, when all this blew up, to know that Aaron had not only been an accomplice to Jacob's downfall, he'd provided an actual voodoo priestess to facilitate it?

The thoughts plagued him until, finally, he fell into a restless sleep.

Where the hell am I?

Aaron slowly took in his surroundings. He was in a lush garden, full of fragrant, blossoming flowers. There was a small set of stone steps, descending toward a flagstone path that led to a huge willow tree. The day was bright, the sky a brilliant cerulean blue with only the mildest scattering of fluffy white clouds. It was summer: he felt the heat of the sun seeping into him like a warm bath.

He headed down the steps, toward the tree. The drooping branches parted.

Mahjani was standing there, looking beautiful enough to make him catch his breath. She was wearing a lacy white sundress that glowed against her dark chocolate skin. Her eyes were low lidded, inviting.

"I always wanted to see you here," she said.

He felt desire curl through him, as it always did. "Where is this place?"

"This is my garden," she explained, holding her hands out. Instinctively, he reached for her. When their palms touched, it was like closing an electrical circuit. He felt the power of their contact like touching a live wire. "I go here when I need to think or rest. This is my special place."

He could tell from the weight of her words that she was entrusting him with something precious, taking him here. He pulled her close, holding her, breathing in the perfume of her, mimosa and ginger and something essentially female.

"Mahjani," he breathed, as his body tightened. "God, I've missed you."

"You were the one that left me," she reproved gently.

"I know." He held her more fiercely. "You know I had my reasons."

She nodded. "Your family."

"They never would have accepted you," he said, blurting out the truth he didn't even want to admit to himself. "They already think that I'm . . ."

"Less than they are, because of your emotional side," she said, and he felt her shrug against him. "You know I don't agree with that. You're a grown man, Aaron. You're old enough to make your own choices, without worrying what your family or what anyone else thinks."

Her comment stung. He didn't release her, though. It had

been too long since he'd had her in his arms, and if it meant listening to her chastise him for his behavior, so be it.

She isn't wrong, anyway.

He closed his eyes, trying to ignore the persistent little voice of his conscience.

"It's not important," she said, to his relief. "That's not why you're here, anyway."

"Why am I here, then?"

She leaned back enough for him to see the lazy smile covering her face. "Why don't I show you?"

With that, she took a step back . . . and undid the string straps that held up the halter top of her dress. With a negligible motion, she let the top slide down, revealing her full breasts.

His cock went hard in a rush. His mouth went dry.

Shimmying slightly, she let the skirt fall away. She wasn't wearing underwear beneath the frothy excuse for a dress, so now she stood, bare and beautiful in the sunlight. Then she opened her arms, half presenting, half inviting.

He needed no further encouragement. Mindlessly, he tore his own clothes off, reaching for her eagerly.

"Mahjani," he murmured, his voice hot against her skin. He kissed her fiercely, his hands roaming over her frame in hungry indecision. What to touch first? Her wonderful, generous breasts? The curving span of her hips? Or the luscious triangle beckoning to him between her thighs?

She tugged him down to the ground. The lawn was thick and lush, soft as velvety moss, downy as a cloud. They tumbled and rolled for a moment, laughing playfully. She nipped at his earlobe, revealing the sensitive spot that he'd never realized he possessed until she discovered it. Her rounded fingernails traced lightly down his chest before reaching down and circling his erection, stroking the shaft, cupping his balls and massaging them until he groaned, his eyes all but crossing with desire.

"Mahjani, I have to be inside you," he growled, pinning her against the soft grass.

Her laugh was like a rippling stream. "I need to feel you inside me," she answered huskily. "As you say—it's been too long."

He felt her legs shift beneath him, her thighs spreading wide. His cock nudged at her wet curls, bluntly nosing for her opening. He reached between them, his breath ragged, as he positioned himself. Then he pressed forward, groaning loudly as he felt her wet, warm pussy sheath him tightly.

"Mahjani." He stayed still inside her for a moment, shivering with the intensity of pleasure that flooded his system. "Baby, you're so fucking tight, I want to stay like this forever."

"Really?" With a note of challenge, she tilted her hips upward, her pussy undulating around his cock shaft.

"Maybe not," he joked back, withdrawing slowly, patiently, the way he remembered she liked it. Then he pressed forward, still at that slow pace. Sweat trickled down his chest as he continued his patient thrusts.

"Aaron," she whimpered, her hips wriggling and writhing beneath the sensual onslaught. She caressed her own breasts, a sight that never ceased to arouse him, fanning the flames of his passion even further. His speed increased unwittingly as his body started to respond to her cues. He forced himself to back down, keep control.

Her breathing was sharp and staccato, her hips starting to pump against him in impatient bursts. Her head lolled back and forth, her eyes closed. She cried out, a long, high-pitched squeal, and he could feel her orgasm massaging his cock. He held on, determined not to give in just yet.

It's been too long, he echoed mentally. He was going to enjoy this as long as he possibly could.

When her shudders of pleasure subsided, he gently nudged her over onto her knees. She moved willingly, purring with satisfaction. Then he reentered her, moaning softly. The slick wetness of her climax made his entrance a smooth, hot glide. He held her hips, drawing her to him. Then he leaned over her, his stomach touching her back, the rounded softness of her buttocks caressing his thighs. He reached around, cupping and massaging her breasts as his hips moved in measured, deliberate thrusts.

"Every time you make love to me," she said breathlessly, "I feel like I'm going to lose my mind . . . ."

"I've always wanted you," he said, his hips moving a bit faster, a bit deeper. She reared back to meet his every pressing thrust, and he gasped at her enthusiasm. His control slipped, as he felt her hips swaying, drawing his cock deeper, slamming back against him. "Mahjani!"

He lost it. He started plunging into her, and she breathed frantically, wrapping her feet over his calves, arching her back like a cat, screaming with pleasure every time he buried himself in her. He pounded against her as his cock scrambled against the beginning twinges of satisfaction. His orgasm roared through him, leaving him temporarily blank, completely shorted out. His body jerked against her, and he reached forward, rubbing her clitoris as his cock emptied itself in her. She gasped as he found the spot, circling it firmly with his fingertips. He was rewarded with another orgasm from her, squeezing every last drop of come from him.

They collapsed on their sides, his cock still buried deep within her. When he could move, he nuzzled the nape of her neck, his arm around her waist, just below her breasts. He spooned against her.

He couldn't remember the last time he'd felt so content.

She sighed, stroking his arm. "This has been wonderful."

He tightened his hold instinctively. "Don't leave me."

"I have to," she replied, rolling away from him. His penis felt cold and limp without her. He reached for her, but she evaded his grasp. "Aaron, I just need one more thing from you."

"Anything." Now his whole body felt chilled, damp. "Anything at all."

"What is Jacob's phone number?"

He stared at her blankly. "What?"

"His phone number," she repeated patiently. "How can I reach your brother?"

Confused, Aaron rattled off Jacob's cell phone number. She smiled.

"Now you have to wake up, Aaron."

"No," he murmured sadly. "I don't want to leave you."

"You already have," she said, kissing him softly. "Good-bye, Aaron."

He closed his eyes, kissing her back, trying to hold her, but he could already feel the warmth of her lips disappearing. . . .

He opened his eyes.

He was in his room. His bed was wet, stained from his ejaculate. He'd had an orgasm in his sleep.

It was a dream, he thought bitterly, getting up and changing the linens. But it felt so incredibly real. Not just the sex, although that in and of itself was phenomenal. No, it was the feeling of closeness and caring that he'd always reveled in with Mahjani. She never held anything back. To have her leave was like losing her all over again.

And whose fault was that?

The clock said it was 5:00 a.m. No way he was getting back to sleep now. He pulled on some sweats, headed for his kitchen to start his coffeemaker.

His phone rang, surprising him. Who the hell would call at this hour?

"Hello?" he asked tentatively, bracing himself for bad news.

"It's Mahjani."

His body responded like a lit torch. "Mahjani?"

"Don't ever tell me that dreams aren't real again."

There was a click. He stared at the phone in disbelief.

Chapter Eight

"Thank you so much for meeting me, Mahjani," Jacob said.

She nodded regally. Her hair was in long, flowing dread-locks, a strange and warm counterpoint to the light snow falling outside. She had arrived at the Jacquards' house in the Hamptons in a town car, one he'd hired. He'd even gotten her a hotel.

He wasn't sure how long this was going to take, but he wanted her here for the duration. He needed all the help he could get.

"You know, I was actually surprised when you called," he ventured, letting her in the house and taking her coat.

"So was your brother, I'll wager." Her full lips curved into an enigmatic smile.

Jacob cleared his throat. "I haven't really been discuss-ing this with Aaron." Especially not after Aaron's threat and his two-week deadline. "Have you heard of a case like this before?"

Now her expression turned serious. "It's different than the zombie cases I have researched," she said slowly. "Those are deliberate, and they mimic death . . . for a short time, anyway, until the victim is unearthed. Generally, they then wake with no memory of their past life."

Jacob frowned. "I seem to remember that," he mused. "Some scientists were experimenting with the blowfish toxins, trying to come up with new pharmaceuticals. They still don't know why the voodoo powder works."

She nodded, and Jacob thought her expression looked a little triumphant. "Science can't explain everything, Doctor White."

It sounded like she wasn't simply talking to him.

He sighed. "I realize that, believe me."

She patted his hand. "Let me see her," she said. "And we'll see what I can do."

He took her to Rory's room. She looked startled, put off by the medical equipment no doubt. She reached forward, her long, delicate fingers tracing over Rory's face. She then surprised Jacob by taking Rory's pulse. "She just looks like she's taking a nap," Mahjani marveled.

"I said the same thing, the first time I saw her."

Mahjani closed the door, then crossed her arms. "You're in love with her."

Now he was the one who started. "What . . . how . . . ?"

"It's obvious, if you know what you're looking for," she said. "And if what you told me on the phone was true—if you're able to enter her dreams, with no prior relationship with her—then I would say that there's a definite bond between you two."

In any other circumstance, he would be scoffing at Mahjani's musings, both on voodoo and the thought of a fated, destined "love." But since he'd met Rory, nothing in his past life applied. He nodded instead. "Yes," he croaked. "I am in love with her."

She looked satisfied with his answer. "This is powerful magic," she said, waving her hands slowly over Rory's inert form. "I only know of a handful of *boktors* capable of this kind of evil."

"I'm sorry. What was that word?"

Mahjani looked up at him momentarily. "*Boktor.* It's an evil priest or priestess. Someone willing to use the loas for dangerous, destructive magic."

He nodded. Loas, he knew . . . he'd picked up several books on voodoo, trying to arm himself as best he could with knowledge from experts. Loas were spirits, intermediaries between the living and the dead. They weren't gods, but they were far more powerful than humans, if the literature was to be believed.

"I know who did this to her, though," he said absently. "I'm just trying to figure out a way to reverse—"

"Wait a minute," Mahjani interrupted. "You *know*?"

"I've seen her, in the dreams. Her name is Serafina, and . . ." He stopped when he saw Mahjani visibly turn ashen. "What? What is it?"

"Tall woman? Long hair, worn in braids? Mocha skin?"

When he nodded, she wrung her hands. "You said that Rory took a vacation to the Caribbean."

"Her parents lived there, too," he added.

"Saint Genevieve." She said the island's name like a curse. "Serafina Montenegro. If Rory crossed paths with this woman, somehow—"

"Not Rory. At least, not exactly. Her parents struck a deal with Serafina. I get the impression that they did not hold up their end of the bargain."

Mahjani's mouth formed a thin, straight line. "I will need to talk to them."

Jacob squirmed uncomfortably. "Is it necessary?" Bad enough that he needed to call in a voodoo priestess to consult. But to let the Jacquards know . . .

"Do you want Rory to wake or not?"

The words made his back straighten. "I'll get her parents for you."

Minutes later, Mrs. Jacquard met Jacob and Mahjani in Rory's room. "Who is this?" she asked, her voice still pleasant, even though her eyes were curious.

"This is . . . a colleague of mine. Mahjani Rafallo." He watched as the two women shook hands, ignoring Mahjani's warning glare. "She's going to be helping me with Rory's treatment."

"Do you think there's any hope, Doctor Rafallo?" Mrs. Jacquard asked, in the same quietly desperate tone she had once asked Jacob.

"I'm not a doctor," Mahjani replied. "And there is always hope. I will need to ask you some questions, though."

At Mahjani's admission, Mrs. Jacquard looked confused. "All right," she said. "Questions about what?"

"About your interactions with a woman named Serafina, when you lived in Saint Genevieve."

Jacob watched as the older woman weaved, leaning against a chair for support. His arms shot out, catching her before she could faint. Her pupils were dilated in fear.

"How did you know?" she demanded. "How did you know!"

Mahjani shook her head. "I am a vodun priestess. I live in New York—"

"You," Mrs. Jacquard said, glaring at Jacob. "*You* let this woman into my house. Oh, God, if Henri finds out, he will be furious!"

"What bargain did you strike with Serafina?" Mahjani continued, with all the relentlessness of a police interrogator. "What price were you supposed to pay?"

Mrs. Jacquard's mouth worked silently, like a dying fish. She looked at Jacob for some kind of support. Her eyes were gray, like Rory's, he noticed, and for a second he felt a wave of sympathy for the woman. Then he looked at Mahjani. He shook his head.

Mrs. Jacquard collapsed further in his arms. "I'm not going to talk about this in front of her," she said, nodding her head at Rory. "We'll talk in the sitting room."

She leaned heavily on Jacob as he accompanied her to the sitting room, Mahjani following close behind. She sat in one of the high-backed armchairs. Mahjani sat next to her, on the nearby divan. Jacob hovered.

"If you could pour me a glass . . . ?" Mrs. Jacquard gestured to the cut-crystal decanter of brandy. He poured two fingerlengths in a snifter, handing it to her.

She downed almost the entire amount in a long swallow. Then she coughed, painfully, handing him the empty glass.

"Henri always loved Saint Genevieve," Mrs. Jacquard said quickly, not looking either Jacob or Mahjani in the eye. "He had vacationed there with his family, as a boy. His life's dream was to open a five-star resort on the island, and he did. We were rich, we were happily married and in love. The only thing that marred our lives was that we couldn't have a child." She sounded so melancholy, Jacob's chest squeezed painfully. "Rory was the crowning gift, everything we could have ever wanted. I thought I would give anything to have her."

"What, exactly, did you give?" Mahjani pressed.

Finally, Mrs. Jacquard met Mahjani's gaze. "We were supposed to introduce Serafina to our rich friends," she said. "She was well known in the Caribbean. She wanted to be richer, famous, I guess."

Mahjani nodded in understanding.

"When we didn't, she cursed Rory." The look of remembered horror was clear on Mrs. Jacquard's face as she admitted this in a tortured whisper.

"Do you remember exactly how the curse went?" Mahjani prompted.

Mrs. Jacquard shook her head. "I only know that Rory would have a happy childhood, but she would never become a woman without dying."

Mahjani's breath hitched. "I see."

The door slammed, and Mr. Jacquard stalked into the room. "What the hell's going on here?"

Jacob moved to intercept him. "Mr. Jacquard—"

To his shock, the older man shoved him. "Who the hell is this?" He pointed at Mahjani.

Jacob frowned. "This is Mahjani Rafallo. She's an expert in voodoo and—"

Before he could finish his sentence, Mr. Jacquard surprised him with a quick punch, rocking his head back. Jacob's hands bunched into fists as the pain in his jaw intensified, but he stopped himself before he counterattacked.

"Get her out of this house."

Mahjani stood gracefully. "It's all right, Jacob," she said, in her quiet voice. "I think I've learned all I need to."

Now Mr. Jacquard stepped closer to Mahjani, his face menacing. "If you tell anyone about my daughter, or anything my wife might have told you, I will make sure that your life is ruined. Do you understand?"

Jacob reached for the man, grabbing him away from Mahjani. "You'll leave her alone," Jacob threatened.

Mahjani sighed. "I was just leaving, sir," she said instead, putting a hand on Jacob's arm. "Jacob, if you could walk me to the car?"

Jacob and Mr. Jacquard's eyes locked, glaring, challenging. Finally, Jacob stepped away, escorting Mahjani to the foyer, helping her with her coat. They took a step out into the crisp winter air.

"I'm sorry," Jacob said. "I had no idea they'd react like this."

"It's all right," Mahjani said, unperturbed. "He feels responsible for what happened to Rory. In a way, he's right to. But I wouldn't wish this on my worst enemy. He gets to be firsthand witness to his daughter's pain and imprisonment every day."

Put that way, Jacob felt a little more empathy for the sour man.

"I need to research this a little further," Mahjani added, opening the door to the town car. "Call me at the hotel later. I will have a ritual planned out. And, now that I've met her, I think I will be able to meet you both in this dreamworld—if you'll allow it."

He nodded. "Anything you need."

With that, she closed the door. The car drove away.

When he reentered the house, Rory's parents were waiting for him. Mrs. Jacquard looked miserable. Mr. Jacquard simply looked furious.

"I thought you were a reputable doctor," Mr. Jacquard accused. "What were you thinking, bringing that . . . that *charlatan* here? To see Rory? I should fire you right now!"

Jacob felt a stab of panic, but kept his face set. "I'm pursuing angles that other doctors haven't," he pointed out.

"You're making a mockery of her illness," Mr. Jacquard said sharply. "You're—"

"Do you want Rory to wake up or not?"

The sentence that Mahjani had thrown at him worked equally well on Mr. Jacquard, momentarily stunning him. Finally, he chuffed loudly.

"This isn't a solution, this is a fraud," he said, although

his voice was far less certain. "If I find out she's been in this house again, I'll not only have you fired and kicked out, I'll have your license. Don't fuck with me."

Jacob nodded, then watched as the older man stomped off to his study. When it was quiet, he turned to Mrs. Jacquard.

"Are you all right?"

She nodded, her eyes bright with unshed tears. "He won't forgive me," she said. "He'll never forgive me."

Jacob didn't say anything. He waited.

"Is there anything else you need to know from me, Doctor White?"

He took a deep breath. "Did you talk to Serafina?" he asked quietly. "Did . . . did you try to get her to reverse the spell?"

"Of course." Now the tears spilled over, and she dabbed at them with a linen handkerchief. "Don't you think I would? When Rory fell, I was ready to sign over my entire bank account. I was ready to throw her a promotional party at the Four Seasons. But there was no use."

"She wouldn't negotiate?"

Mrs. Jacquard's laugh was watery. "You misunderstand me," she said.

Jacob's brow furrowed.

"Serafina was dead when I returned to the island."

Rory heard Jacob's footsteps before she saw him. "I scavenged as best I could from what's left of the hotel," she called to the mouth of the cave. "There wasn't much, but—"

She stopped abruptly. Jacob was there—but he wasn't alone. A black woman with dreadlocks and a pretty sundress was standing next to him.

"Rory," Jacob said, "I'd like you to meet Mahjani. She's a voodoo priestess from Manhattan, and a . . . friend of my brother's."

Mahjani held out a hand, her eyes a kind, velvety brown as she met Rory's surprised gaze. "It's a pleasure to meet you."

Rory shook her hand, glad that she'd put on her clothes to rummage in the charred hulk of the hotel. "A friend of Jacob's brother," she said slowly. "Does that mean you're . . . ?"

"Real?" Mahjani finished, nodding, the hint of a smile playing around her lips. "Yes. Jacob found me so I could help you."

"Can you help me?"

"We'll see," she said, nodding. "First of all, we can't let Serafina know I'm here. That Jacob breached this world is the reason I'm able to enter—and it's the reason why Serafina's ghost is so angry with you."

"Ghost?"

Jacob stepped next to Rory, putting an arm around her shoulders. "I just found out today," he murmured, giving her a comforting squeeze. "Serafina died before you fell into your coma."

"Then who have I seen?"

Mahjani took that one. "Her ghost is living in your dream-world," Mahjani explained. "It's a powerful curse, and when she died, I think that she had one of her acolytes move her spirit with yours. She's always held a piece of your spirit, from the time you were conceived. That's how she's had such power over you and your family."

Rory felt her head spinning.

"So what we've got to do is get you out of this false dream-world, out of her power," Mahjani continued. "She's kept you trapped here, as a child, so she has a place to stay while she figures out another way to remain immortal."

"I'm not a child," Rory protested.

"A figure of speech," Mahjani said gently. "You were performing a rite of passage when you fell into your coma. From what Jacob has told me, your coma—and, at the moment, your recovery—all seem linked to sex."

Rory felt her cheeks heat with a blush. She nodded quickly. "I suppose."

Mahjani pursed her lips thoughtfully. "We're going to need to teach you that you have power here," she said. "We're going to need to harness that power, and perform a ritual in front of the loas—the spirits—to prove that you are your own person and that Serafina no longer has any hold over you."

"How do I do that?"

"By performing a sex ritual."

Rory blanched. "Have sex, in front of those—those *things*?"

Now Mahjani frowned. "If you don't respect those 'things,' as you call them, then you have no chance whatsoever of leaving this place," she said crisply. "They are spirits, and they are to be revered for their power."

Rory nodded, chastened. "Still, to have sex, in front of them . . ."

"I agree," Jacob said. "Isn't there another way?"

"What would you suggest?" Mahjani asked, her expression amused.

Jacob took a deep breath. "I could get rid of Serafina."

Rory gasped. Jacob's expression grew harsher.

"She's threatening the life of the woman I love," he said, and his voice was like a razor. "She's threatening me. If it comes down to that, I can and will destroy her."

"No," Mahjani said, before Rory could ruminate too long on Jacob's statement. "Killing Serafina might kill Rory, as well. Once we free Rory, Serafina's soul will die, and no longer be a danger to either of you. As far as I can see, the ritual is the only chance you have."

Rory looked at Jacob, then leaned against him. His solidity and warmth reassured her, as did the arm he quickly placed around her shoulders. "All right," Rory said, with quiet determination. "Tell me what we have to do."

"You two are going to need to learn to have sex."

Rory spluttered. Jacob chuckled softly.

"I think we've got that one covered," he murmured.

Mahjani shook her head. "No, no. I'm not talking about frantic fumblings and animalistic mating. This must be a sacred act. In spiritual practice, this would fall under the category of tantra: using kundalini energy to raise incredible power."

Rory bit her lip. "The last time I saw Serafina, in her grove," she said slowly, "she was—having sex, with two men. Is that what she was doing?"

Mahjani sighed. "She was performing a version of that,

yes. She probably was channeling the loa of Erzuli, the spirit of romantic love and feminine beauty."

"Erzuli," Rory interrupted. "I remember that."

"Erzuli is powerful—and temperamental. She is very vain and wants many different partners." Mahjani tapped her bottom lip with her fingertips, her expression thoughtful. "I think that we're going to call a different loa for you. Oshun."

"Oshun?" Jacob repeated.

"Oshun is the spirit of harmony," Mahjani explained. "She represents beauty, love, and ecstasy. Her love isn't as fickle as Erzuli's. She's the patron of marriage."

"Marriage." Rory rolled the word over in her mind—then surreptitiously sneaked a look at Jacob.

He was staring at her, a considering smile hovering around his lips.

"To perform the sex ritual for Oshun, you are going to need to consider yourself . . . *hmmm.* This is difficult to explain." Mahjani looked around the cave. "Better to show you. I think I'll be able to risk a little power without exposing myself to Serafina's wrath."

She closed her eyes. Then the surroundings shimmered.

The ground was covered in a thick, fleecy wool. There was a purple square of satin in the center of the floor. There was also a table covered with foodstuffs and a closed wooden chest.

"I'm going to need you two to get naked and lie on the square of purple cloth," Mahjani instructed.

"Naked?" Rory gulped.

"You've been naked together numerous times," Mahjani pointed out.

"Not with an audience!"

"I won't be an audience," Mahjani said in a soothing voice. "I will be your teacher, your guidance. You're going to need to trust me."

Rory bit her lip painfully. Then she started to peel off her clothes, not looking at Mahjani as she got down to bare skin. Jacob was grinning slightly, but he was only looking at Rory.

Mahjani nodded encouragingly as Rory and Jacob both knelt on the purple cloth. "The important part of this ritual is the focus and the reverence," she said. Her voice was both comforting and instructive, which reassured Rory. "You will focus on this act as if you've never had sex before. You will both become sacred—a sex god and a sex goddess, for lack of a better term. When you learn this, it won't matter if I'm in the room, or if an entire football stadium was watching you. All that will matter is each other and what you're feeling. All right?"

"All right," Rory responded, and Jacob nodded, still staring at her.

"Now," Mahjani said, reaching into the wooden chest. "I'm going to blindfold you both."

Rory was startled, but she didn't comment. The blindfold was black velvet, soft against her skin, although it was tied tight enough that she couldn't see anything. Her breathing increased in speed, and she reached out blindly. Her fingertips met Jacob's much larger hand, and he held tight, giving her a squeeze.

"All right. Now, I want you both to start breathing, slowly, to my count. You'll be breathing in time, together."

Rory obediently followed Mahjani's instruction, hearing Jacob's even, matching breathing across from her. He still held her hand.

"Now, I want you to say what you cherish about each other," Mahjani prompted. "Don't be glib—this is important."

Rory paused, thinking. "I cherish your strength," she said, the words coming out in a near whisper. "I think I've been so afraid all my life, of doing the wrong thing, getting hurt, getting in trouble—I feel brave when I'm with you."

He squeezed her hand again. "I cherish your vulnerability," he responded. "You're the most open, accepting woman I've ever met, and the only one I've ever loved."

"You're the only man I've ever loved," she answered, her heart in her throat.

"This is an excellent start," Mahjani interjected. "Now, I want you to lie down on the satin square, next to each other but not touching. At least not yet."

Rory moved blindly, bumping against Jacob's warm skin. She giggled, more nerves than humor. Even an inch away, she could still feel the heat of his body. Her own nipples puckered and tightened.

"I'm going to be working on heightening your senses," Mahjani whispered. Her soothing voice seemed to float above them, disembodied. "Just relax, get into the feel of it."

Music started to play: something gentle, almost arabesque sounding. Rory sniffed experimentally. The air was perfumed with something, both subtle and smoky. Incense, she reasoned, then sniffed again. Rose and sandalwood. It smelled nice. With the music and the incense, she started to relax.

She felt a light touch on her back, then down one arm. It was heavenly soft. "What is that?" she asked reflexively.

"*Shhhh,*" Mahjani said. "It's chinchilla. Just focus on the sensations."

Rory sighed as she felt the ultrasoft fur stroke over her stomach. She tensed only slightly as the softness brushed over her erect nipples. Then, the furry glove was pressed in her hand.

"Now, caress Jacob with it."

Rory did as requested, reaching for Jacob, stroking whatever part of him she could find. Was that an arm? His leg? His torso? It didn't matter. She recognized his shoulder, stroked up to his neck, brushed a caress against his chin. She felt his lips press a hot kiss against the inner flesh of her wrist, and she shivered, smiling.

"Now your turn, Jacob," Mahjani said.

Rory put down the fur mitt, waiting for him to brush her with it. Instead, she heard him gasp lightly, and wondered what was going on.

"It's an ostrich feather," Mahjani said. "Do you like it?"

Jacob's response was a strangled moan. Rory felt immediately like tearing off the blindfold and seeing what was happening. His moans were soft, but intense.

"Now stroke Rory."

Rory felt the delicious whisper of the feather along her thighs, over her stomach, over her face. She laughed as it tickled her ear.

They continued that way for some time, feeling a multitude of textures, rubbing them along each other: the almost liquid softness of flower petals, the downy texture of raw cotton, and the slow strokes of a sable brush. By the time they were done, Rory felt like every nerve ending was tingling, completely alive.

"Now, you're going to repeat the process," Mahjani said. "Only you're going to be touching each other, and yourselves, with your hands . . . and with this new awareness."

Rory reached out, feeling for Jacob. When her palms contacted with his skin, she felt his skin as though she'd never touched him before. His skin was hot, yet smooth: she could feel the flex and play of muscles beneath, like cords of iron beneath satin. She smoothed her hands lower, tracing the planes of his sides, his abdomen . . . feeling the smooth sprinkling of hair grow thicker, until she reached the springy mass of pubic hair, then the heated smoothness of his penis. She ran her fingertips along his cock, marveling at the amazing texture, so impossibly soft over such a hard organ. His cock head was like velvet, with moisture at the tip.

She felt his hands tracing over hers, almost tentatively. "You're so soft," he marveled. "Like . . . cream." His hands moved over her face, tracing her blindfold, stroking her cheeks. His fingertip smoothed over her lips. Then his hands moved, skimming over her throat, caressing her collarbone. Gently cupping her breasts, his thumbs tracing the roundness of her areolae. She sighed, arching her back, pressing herself more intently into his hands as her fingertips circled his cock.

"Rory," he murmured, and she felt his hips move closer to her.

"Not yet."

Rory moved away, startled. She'd almost forgotten Mahjani was there. The music was still playing, dreamy and drowsy and sexy. The air was scented with beads of jasmine water.

"Time for some sustenance," Mahjani murmured. She chanted softly, and Rory had the impression of a surge of power. "Here we are—food freshly created."

Rory felt something press against her lips. She parted them, taking an experimental bite. "Strawberry," she murmured.

"*Mmmm*," Mahjani said. "Simply taste. Feel it entirely."

Rory felt another piece of food pass her lips. A dolma, some kind of spiced meat wrapped in a grape leaf. The taste was piquant yet hearty. She chewed slowly. She heard Jacob sampling things from Mahjani, as well.

"Now, feed each other."

Rory reached blindly along the ground, touching the platter. She felt the fuzzy skin of a peach. Reaching farther, her fingers dipped in something frothy. She licked her finger. Sweet, light-as-air whipped cream. She experimented further. Chocolate mousse. Tiny quiches. Savory little dumplings.

Holding a peach slice dipped in the cream, she reached for Jacob, feeling for his mouth. When she found it, she fed it to him, slowly. He sighed with appreciation. Then she felt his fingers, groping for her mouth. She opened it willingly.

The tanginess of an orange was enhanced by the richness of a coffee-infused dark chocolate sauce. She moaned softly, licking her lips . . . and his finger.

Next, she felt him take her hand, then dip it in a liquid. Then she felt as he stroked her hand down his chest. She waited, then leaned forward, smelling the chocolaty sauce. She licked his chest, lapping at him like a cat.

He guided her fingers again, this time leading them to the whipped cream . . . then stroking her fingers over his cock.

She tasted him with a smile, enjoying the counterpoint of sweet against his spicy masculinity. He groaned softly when she took him in her mouth.

When she released him, she felt his hands, wet with something, massaging her breasts, her stomach. Then, his hot, searching mouth devoured every inch of her skin. She gasped and writhed beneath his thorough tasting. Then, she felt him part the lips of her labia, then stroke her most delicate skin with something cool, juicy, and fuzzy. The peach slice, she realized.

When he replaced the slice with his mouth, drinking in its juices, she came like a gunshot.

"This is the best flavor of them all," he said, his breath warming her thighs.

"Jacob," she said, in a hitching breath. "Jacob . . ."

She altered their angle, shifting so that she could feel his cock, positioned at her head while his head remained between her thighs.

"Wait," Mahjani's voice interrupted.

Rory didn't want to wait. She made an impatient, hoarse sound in the back of her throat.

The blindfold came off, and for a moment, Rory was blind, adjusting to the light. Then she looked around her.

The platters of food were moved off to the side. The cave was drenched in the warm candlelight of hundreds of votive candles, each in a holder of a semi-precious stone, glistening in rich jewel tones. The incense wafted in a looping cloud, and there was a music box playing delicately. Mahjani stood in the shadows, her eyes dark yet luminous. She was only wearing a filmy nightgown, and her breasts were erect, as well.

Rory looked at Jacob. His cock was presented in all its huge, erect glory, right in front of her face. She glanced down. He was staring at her pussy like it was the best gift he'd ever received. He licked his lips. They were both sticky and slick with food: she was wet with orgasm. For a second, she felt a moment's apprehension.

What am I doing?

"Just feel," Mahjani's voice drifted over to her.

Rory reached out for Jacob's reassuring warmth. He leaned forward, his fingers reaching for her clit, massaging it back to its prior erect state. She shivered and moaned softly, her muscles pliable as clay. She opened her mouth, sucking on the tip of his cock as she felt the rough-soft texture of his balls in the palm of her hand.

He replaced his fingertips with his mouth, sucking on her clit, roughing it with the edges of his teeth. She gasped, suckling more intently. He pressed one finger inside her pussy, and she took him deep enough into her mouth to gag.

Suddenly, their lovemaking moved like rushing water: she could feel him writhing against her, tasted his salty, smooth cock as he lapped at her clit, smelled the rich scent of their lovemaking as her skin tingled with strange, overwhelming waves of desire. He came in her mouth as she orgasmed, and she tasted the tangy shot of his come, lapping it up eagerly, tracing the fissure of his cock with her tongue as he shuddered and moaned against her wet cunt.

They rolled away from each other, on their backs, staring at the candlelit cave ceiling. The world seemed brighter, more intensely colored. Rory took a deep breath.

Suddenly Mahjani appeared from the shadows.

"I think," she murmured thoughtfully, "that you're ready."

Chapter Nine

Mahjani sat in the office attached to her classroom at NYU, poring over some old texts she'd purchased in Haiti. The handwriting was barely legible. She carefully transcribed a step into her computer.

"Light the black candle, put out the raw rum mixed with sugarcane," she muttered as she typed. Then she rubbed at her pounding temples. She'd been working on this ritual for the past few hours, since her last class was dismissed. It was already dark out: the ceremonial masks and paintings she'd gathered, as well as her small altar, looked ominous in the fading light. She'd stay here till midnight or later, if she had to. Jacob wanted to perform the ritual tonight, but there was simply too much to prepare: the right herbs, the drawings, how they were going to handle the animal sacrifice. The fact that she would have to write everything out for Jacob to do by himself only made things harder. If he missed a step . . . if anything went wrong . . .

She frowned, her fingers hitting the keyboard with more force than necessary. Nothing would go wrong. The girl's life, and Jacob's, depended on it.

She barely registered footsteps entering her classroom. When her office door shut, she jumped, her heart pounding. Her hand reached reflexively for a long, curved ceremonial knife.

Aaron stood at the doorway, in the heavy shadows made by her small desk light. "You wouldn't use that thing on me, would you?"

"I could." She took a deep breath, trying to calm the rush of adrenaline that still caused her body to scramble. "I still might. What are you doing here?"

"You haven't been answering my calls."

"I've been busy." She gestured to the piles of papers and books strewn around her office. "I'm still busy, so . . ."

"This will only take a minute." He stepped closer to her. "Why did you call me the other morning?"

She grimaced. Calling him after their dream contact had been an act of pure ego—a "fuck you" to his logical, well-ordered mind. She'd known that it would drive him crazy. However, she also should have realized that he wouldn't be able to let it go.

"I was awake, thinking about how we'd left things," she said, not entirely lying. "I was angry with you, so I called. Chalk it up to poor impulse control." That was also true.

He stared at her, his blue eyes like incandescent torches. "That's it?"

She sensed his hesitation, and that same angry, mischievous spirit nudged her to taunt him. "Why? I can't imagine you coming all this way just to ask me about a crank call."

Was she imagining, or did he redden slightly? A small part of her felt a drop of glee at his discomfort. "I was having a dream about you," he said. "What with the timing, and the way we broke up, and the stress I've been feeling about Jacob . . . I should have known you weren't really calling me because of anything specific."

Now guilt pierced through her triumph. "I'm sorry I called."

"I'm not."

He took a step closer to her desk, and she stood quickly, retreating, unsure of his mood. "I guess we don't have anything else to talk about," she stammered.

He closed the distance between them. "Guess not."

With that, he leaned down, kissing her hard as his hands grasped her upper arms, pulling her to him.

She gasped against his mouth. He'd always been a passionate lover, but refined, sophisticated. This was different. He felt wild, unrestrained. He wasn't seducing her. He was *taking* her.

She felt a thrill as he leaned her against the wall, his mouth slanting over hers punishingly. Pinning her against the wall with his body, his hands moved from her arms to her breasts, caressing them through the thick wool of her suit jacket. He undid the buttons, massaging the purple silk blouse beneath. When he reached the buttons of her blouse, she expected him to tug at them impatiently, get slowed down by them.

He ripped the blouse open, his hand cupping her breast and gently squeezing the nipple.

"Aaron." She should protest, but the sensation of him, wanting her so badly, only fueled the fire that she'd been feeling since she visited him in the dream, giving in to her own longing. She reached down between them, yanking open his fly, roughly opening the zipper. She reached under the waistband of the boxers, feeling the hard heat of his cock spearing up toward her. She yanked down the boxers, letting his cock spring free.

He tugged down the bra cup, taking her nipple into his mouth and giving it a long, hard, loving taste. She bumped her head against the wall as she threw her head back in abandon. She kicked her shoes off and hiked her skirt up around her waist. He peeled her stockings off roughly, tearing them, removing them and her panties with frenzied haste as her hips wiggled enticingly, trying to help him.

She couldn't remember ever feeling so hot. His pants were around his thighs, his cock jutting at her, and she lifted one leg, hooking it over his hip, rubbing her pussy against him hungrily. He gripped her other leg, lifting it, encouraging her to wrap her legs around his waist for balance as he plunged inside her with one powerful thrust. He groaned loudly, and she held her breath at the overwhelming feeling of being filled.

The dream had been incredible. This, though . . . this was better.

This was *real*.

He started rocking against her, crushing her against the wall as his cock delved farther and farther inside her willing cunt. Gasping, writhing, she gyrated in ecstasy, grinding her clit against the stone-hard shaft of him, doing her own private lap dance as he held her hips, pulling her flush against his abdomen. The head of his cock brushed against her G-spot, and she cried out, biting him on the shoulder, murmuring incoherent pants of desire and encouragement. He flexed his thighs, moving upward with increasing force, sucking on her neck hard enough to leave bruises. The slight, sharp pain was an unbelievable counterpoint to the nameless pleasure that his cock was delivering, and she held the nape of his neck against her, her eyes closed, her hips tilting and retreating, beckoning him as deep as she could take him.

The first orgasm slammed through her, and she couldn't help herself—she screamed his name, her hands clawing down his jacket, her legs tightening around his hips like a vise.

"I'm not through with you yet," he growled against her flesh, and with that, he turned away from the wall, holding her balanced, impaled on his still-hard rod. With one arm, he swept the texts and papers off of her broad desk, laying her on it. The desk was the perfect height. Looking up, she could see him hovering over her, his eyes glowing as he stared at her. His hips continued their relentless tempo, pummeling into her. He reached down, throwing her torn blouse open wider, then leaned over to suck her already erect nipples through the lacy material. The change in angle made him withdraw further, and she whimpered, her hips rising to gain more of him.

Responding, he pushed himself flush again, then reached down between them, his broad thumb seeking and finding the rock-hard nubbin of her clit. He deftly massaged it, going in circular motions, tickling and taunting with just the right pressure.

A second, then a third, orgasm. She arched her back on the desk, almost floating over the surface.

She had been "possessed" by spirits, in rituals, many times. This was the first time she was ever truly possessed by another human being. He had entered her, and now whatever he wanted, she would do. She had no desire but to bring him, and therefore herself, a depth of pleasure she hadn't understood existed.

"That's it, baby," he crooned, and he slowed, withdrawing almost fully, then plunging back inside her before she could protest his leaving. He repeated the process, the stroking friction against the opening of her now incredibly sensitive pussy eliciting shudders throughout her entire body. He licked the cleavage between her breasts, massaging her hips, his cock moving in shallow circles, first clockwise, then counterclockwise. She felt the orgasm starting to build again.

Before she could come, he lifted her left leg up, against his shoulder, allowing him even deeper access. She gasped, straining, arching against him. He entered her deeply, and her whole cunt contracted against him in wave after wave of release.

His speed intensified, until he was moving in rapid rhythm, sliding in and out of her, their bodies making a soft *slap-slap-slap* beneath their hard and heavy breathing, their mutual moans and cries of sexual pleasure. She felt the hot spurt of him inside her, and her body shuddered, lapping it up eagerly as he pounded against her, shuddering with his release. Then he let go of her leg and collapsed on top of her. As they breathed in staggered, uneven gasps, she could feel the pulse in his cock, pounding out of control, just as her heart was. She held him tightly with arms and legs, not caring that he was crushing her. She only wanted to prolong the closeness as long as she could.

She didn't know how long it was, only that it wasn't long enough when he propped himself up, looking at her. She didn't know what to expect, but she was wary enough to ignore her hopes.

"Mahjani," he said, and to her great relief, he kissed her on the lips, a soft, lingering, tender kiss. She kissed him back, her pussy clenching around his now-decreasing cock. "That was . . . I don't even know how to describe that. Although I will say, if you keep holding me like this, I'm going to want to try it all over again."

"You're more than welcome," she purred, rubbing herself against him. She felt his cock jolt, and she smiled against his chest, wiggling her hips.

"You'll be sore," he said, his tone rueful . . . but his eyes gleaming. *Give him a few minutes,* she thought, *and he'd probably come around.* No pun intended.

He withdrew, and she felt more discomfort at losing his warmth and the sensation of him filling her than she did at their enthusiastic mating. He looked around the room.

"I've made a mess here," he said, sounding embarrassed. She watched with regret as he zipped up his fly, tucking himself away. He glanced at her. "I'll buy you a new blouse."

"If you want," she said, grinning wickedly. "I think I'll keep this, as a memento."

He kissed her again, lingering over it. She stroked his face. "Can I take you out to dinner?"

"I'd love it," she said immediately . . . then her gaze fell on her computer screen. The ritual. Jacob. Poor Rory, trapped and in danger. "Except—I'm sorry, but I've got a ton of work to do tonight."

He nodded, looking withdrawn.

"But tomorrow night, maybe?" she found herself saying.

He brightened, his eyes regaining their gleam. "At my place?"

Her heart thrilled. She nodded.

"Let me at least help you clean all this up," he said.

They laughed as they collected the things that had gone everywhere. She was too nervous to ask him what he might be thinking. Nothing had changed, except that they'd had head-banging, white-hot jungle sex in her office. That wasn't enough to build a relationship on.

Right now, her body didn't care.

"Is there anything I can bring tomorrow?" she asked, as she picked up the remnants of the ritual list she'd been preparing.

"Just yourself," he said. "And maybe some . . ."

He stopped short in front of her computer. His eyes narrowed.

She realized what he was looking at the minute he went silent. *Oh, shit, here we go.*

He turned back to her, the vein in his neck bulging. "Mahjani, what the hell is this? And why is Jacob's name on it?"

She pulled her tattered blouse closed, trying for dignity as a defense against his immediate coldness. "It's not your business."

Aaron grabbed her arm again. There was no passion, no longing this time—only an anger that seared like a branding iron. "Listen to me," he said sharply. "You're going to destroy his life with this. Is that what you want?"

She yanked her hand away. There was nothing seductive about him now, and her own anger began to rise. "I'm trying to save a life," she answered. "Your brother's involved with more trouble than he bargained for. His own life might be at risk if you—"

"His professional life is the only one he cares about," Aaron retorted, interrupting her. "Jacob's not in his right mind at the moment. He's so obsessed with this case, so close to burnout, that he thinks he's in love with a patient, a *comatose* patient, for God's sake. The ethical breach here is staggering. Now you're offering him the means to perform some kind of voodoo ritual, in the girl's home? Do you have her caregiver's support on this?"

"That's none of your business."

"He's the only one who's ever given a damn about me," Aaron replied. "He *is* my business. And I'm guessing you don't have their support."

She didn't answer.

"If they find out, they can make sure he loses his license," Aaron said quietly. "They can probably have him arrested. *You will ruin his life if you do this.*"

She sighed. "From that standpoint, it does sound dire."

"So you'll stop this?"

She shook her head. "I've met the girl, in her dreams. She is in real danger, and her time is running out. I think I've found a way to help her wake up. Jacob knows what he is risking, and he's agreed to continue anyway."

"That is such *bullshit!*"

"It's *not* bullshit!" She shoved him away from her desk, toward the door. Rage filled her like acid. "You didn't mind it when you thought I was just a professor of legends, but when you found out I truly believe the stuff, you dropped me. Then you realize I'm good enough to fuck but not good enough to bring home. And God forbid I might be able to provide a cure that your logical, left-brained PhD-wielding mind can't accept!"

"You haven't proven to me that this stuff has even a passing resemblance to reality," he said derisively.

Her hands itched for the ceremonial knife, but for entirely different reasons. Even though she was basically a peaceful person, she wanted to hurt him as much as he was currently hurting her. Instead, she smiled sharply, like a cat taunting a mouse. "The dream," she said. "I met you in a garden, at the bottom of a set of stone steps. My garden. I was wearing white. We made love on the soft grass. You told me you were sorry, you wanted me back. Remember now?"

He stared at her, his mouth working wordlessly.

"How do you think I knew that?"

"What did you do to me?" he asked instead. "Was it . . . some kind of hypnosis? Did you drug me?"

"I used voodoo," she said proudly. "I used what I believe in. I didn't need anything else. You don't have to believe me, but a small part of you will always wonder *was that real?* And it will haunt you for the rest of your life!"

His face turned red. "How did Jacob get in contact with you?"

"Haven't you heard a thing I've said?" She slammed her palms on her desk. "Get out. Just *get out.*"

"I don't believe in this." He sounded angry—and shaken. "It's impossible."

"No, we're impossible," she said, feeling some of the fury drain out of her, replaced by the waxing tide of regret. "I should have known better. I love you, Aaron. But I can't be with someone who hurts me and disrespects me so blatantly."

He turned pale. "I can't help it if I can't believe in . . . what you believe."

"You don't have to believe in voodoo," she said wearily. "You just had to believe in me."

"Mahjani . . ."

"Go," she said, and turned away from him. "I have a ritual to prepare—and I've wasted enough of my precious time tonight on things that are ultimately useless."

She heard the door creak open, then shut. His footsteps echoed down the long corridor. Dry-eyed, she went back to her computer. Even though her chest ached dully, she refused to focus on it. She'd nurse her wounds another time.

Rory's life was at stake, and Jacob would give up his own life, professional and personal, in order to save her. That was real love.

That was the only thing worth fighting for.

"Carrie, could you come here a minute?"

Carrie the night nurse came in from across the hall, her own private room. "Yes, doctor?"

"When was the last time you had a night off?"

She looked surprised, then glanced at the ceiling, obviously doing some quick mental calculations. "Labor Day, I think. But it's okay," she said hastily. "I knew the constraints of the job going in, and . . . well, considering Rory's state, it's really no hardship." She shrugged. "It's not like she's demanding."

Jacob gritted his teeth. He knew that Carrie wasn't being deliberately callous; to her, Rory was just another patient, someone to clean, move, turn over . . . practically a piece of furniture that she had to tend to. Still, it didn't help his knee-jerk response, especially when Carrie chuckled at the end of her observation.

"Why, doctor?" Carrie asked, her teeth flashing in an inviting smile. "Wondering if I might be free some night?"

For a moment, he stared at her uncomprehendingly, his mind so wrapped up in his plan that he didn't realize she'd misunderstood his intent. "Oh no," he said, a little too hastily. Her back went straight, and she pursed her lips, making her normally cute face look distinctly unattractive. "I'm sorry. It's just—I was thinking, because Rory 'isn't demanding,' as you say . . . perhaps you should take the night off."

"Why?" Carrie repeated.

How to play this? He'd hoped that she'd simply jump at the opportunity—it was a Saturday night, after all. "Surely there are more fun things an attractive girl like yourself would prefer to be doing on a weekend. It's not that late, after all."

Her seductive smile returned, with twice as much force. "Now that you mention it, there *are* more fun things I'd rather do," she said, advancing on him, leaning forward ever so slightly, her eyes homing in on his like guided missiles. "Maybe we could go to your room, discuss it . . ."

He dodged, getting closer to Rory's bed. "I'm really making a mess of this," he said, shaking his head. "I didn't mean . . ."

"Come on, doctor," Carrie said, batting her eyes. At least, it distinctly looked like eye batting. Who did that? "I've seen you naked, after all. I've heard you moaning in your sleep. A man like you, devoted to your work, must get lonely . . ."

He sighed. Any other case, he might have considered taking her up on it. He wouldn't have even thought about her afterward, but simply used the sex as a stress release and then focused back on the case at hand.

God, I was an asshole. Now that he'd finally fallen in love, a lot of other aspects of his life were becoming much clearer. "That's inappropriate," he said, trying a different tack altogether. "We work together. This is our employer's house. I simply wanted to offer you a night of freedom, reward for lots of long nights of hard work."

He watched as the blush of embarrassment flooded her face, and her eyes turned flinty hard. "I see." She glanced at her watch. "It's a bit late for me to call in a replacement, but I suppose . . ."

"I can perform nurse duties for one night, Carrie," he said, trying to reassure her. "I really just wanted to offer you a break. All right?"

She nodded, but her body language was stiff. She was offended. Being rejected from a seduction attempt would do that to a person, he noted.

"If you insist," she said sourly, and with that, she left the room.

He waited for the next half hour, until she left the house. He glanced at his watch. Nine thirty. He had no idea where she was going: he didn't know how much time he had, but considering the way things had ended, he didn't want to press.

Mrs. Jacquard was already asleep. And, to the best of his knowledge, Mr. Jacquard was out of town. That left him, and the house, to himself.

For the first time since he'd taken on the job, he locked Rory's door.

He got the bag of ritual implements that Mahjani had

given him out of hiding and took out the sheaf of papers outlining how the ritual was to be performed.

"Dark, raw rum," he muttered, pulling out a black bottle. "Candles, . . . cornmeal, . . . doll . . . *ugh!* What the hell is this?" He picked out a strange amalgamation of feathers, a leather cord, and what looked like a bone, with an intricate crystal beadwork around the whole thing. There was a small tag on it: "This is a gris-gris. Remove before using."

Whatever else Aaron might have thought about Mahjani, the woman was as methodical as any research scientist Jacob had ever worked with.

Hastily, Jacob reread the instructions. He felt a little strange and guilty, pouring the cornmeal out on the immaculately vacuumed floor, as well as lighting the candles and incense. The housekeeper was going to have a fit when she saw this, he realized ruefully.

"Better to beg forgiveness than ask permission," he quoted wryly, taking a swig of the rum. He almost spit it out, his eyes going wide as the sensation of flame tore down his throat. The alcohol content on this stuff had to be illegal—it tasted like pure wood grain, practically poison. His stomach knotted in protest. He poured a little in a glass and put it on Rory's desk, which acted as a makeshift altar.

I can't believe I'm doing this.

Grimacing, he continued setting up, every now and then pausing to listen at the door. His biggest fear was being interrupted. Mrs. Jacquard was a heavy sleeper, these days, and he had Mr. Jacquard to thank for that. Ever since the last big fight, she'd resorted to resting with sleeping pills.

Whatever else, Jacob hoped for her sake that Rory's recovery might begin to heal some of the wounds in the Jacquard family, as well. He continued with grim determination.

"Papa Legba, I beg of you, help this child open the door to the next world," he recited, tapping lightly on a small drum. He was starting to sweat, even though he didn't think it was all that hot in the room. The instructions said to dance next.

It would help if I had any inkling as to what the hell this is all supposed to accomplish, he thought, rubbing a rivulet of sweat from his forehead. He looked at Rory's comatose form. She still looked beautiful, still untouched. Still comatose.

He swayed over the cornmeal "veve" drawing, a voodoo symbol, still feeling anxious and a little nauseous from the rum. The incense was cloying and sweet. He moved rhythmically, getting into the beat, feeling a little dizzy. He glanced over to his notes, on the table.

Offer the blood sacrifice.

That was going to be a problem. He struggled to focus his eyes. He'd drawn the line at killing an animal, especially in the Jacquards' home. He would do whatever he had to if it meant saving Rory, but he felt sure he could figure out another way.

Taking a ceremonial knife, he carefully looked at his own palm, then made a shallow slice. Blood welled up in the crevice. He squeezed his palm, allowing the blood to drip onto the symbol he'd drawn.

Suddenly, he felt a rush of sensation, then numbness, as if

he were staring at the scene from through a video camera. He felt . . . disconnected.

He started to dance, crazily, laughing in a low, weird undertone. He knew at some level that the activity would probably wake someone, but he couldn't stop himself. He walked over to where Rory was sleeping, looking her over, peering at her face through squinted eyes.

"I know this girl." His voice wasn't his own. It sounded old, yet young, with a definite undercurrent of mischief. "She needs passage back, then?"

Yes, Jacob thought to himself, wondering what was going on.

"Need a proper sacrifice, proper ritual," the voice continued critically. "The door can be opened, but only the truly dedicated can go through."

He touched Rory's throat with his sliced hand, leaving a tiny smear of blood. There was a rap on the door.

"Doctor White?" It was Mrs. Jacquard's concerned whisper. "Doctor White, is everything all right?"

Jacob tried to answer her, but couldn't. Instead, he continued crooning, and drinking the dark, strong rum, which now had no effect on him.

"Open this door *now*."

Damn it. Mr. Jacquard. How had that happened?

It had gone too far and was far too late to stop now. Jacob continued moving, swaying, braying with laughter as he cavorted around the symbol. He felt an energy coursing through him, starting from the soles of his feet and spiraling up toward his head. He felt expansive.

The door opened with a crash, the molding of the door frame crumpling off. A beefy security guard stood with the Jacquards, Mr. Jacquard in a suit, Mrs. Jacquard owl-eyed in her nightgown.

"Get him out of here," Mr. Jacquard said. "I'll have your license for this. If I find out you touched her, I'll have your *life*."

Jacob felt the energy immediately snap away to nothing. Whatever had been controlling him left with it. He shook his head, dazed. "It's not what it . . ."

He stopped. Actually, it was *exactly* what it looked like.

"I haven't touched her," he said. "You can have her examined, if you like. I'm just trying an alternate therapy."

"Are you sure I can't have him arrested?" Mr. Jacquard snapped at the security guard.

He shrugged. "You can call the cops, but they'll probably tell you what I told you: unless you've got proof the guy did something besides being weird, it's not gonna be an easy sell."

Mr. Jacquard stared daggers at Jacob. "This isn't over," he said. "If I catch you within a hundred feet of this house, I'll . . . I'll kill you myself!"

"Now, now," the security guard said wearily. "I'll escort this guy off the grounds. *Personally*."

Mr. Jacquard nodded, his eyes still blazing. Mrs. Jacquard's eyes misted, her expression one of utter betrayal. "How could you?" she murmured.

Jacob was then grabbed and hauled bodily outside. The security guard all but dragged him to his car. "You're some piece of work, you know that?" the guard said, shaking his head. "Pretty kid like that, no way she could fight, you probably thought you'd gotten the sweetest deal of your life."

"It's not like that," Jacob protested, but before he could continue, the hulking guard's fist plowed straight into his stomach. He remained standing, but the pain was intense.

"Yeah, well, we'll see what the cops have to say," the guard replied. "I think they couldn't arrest you tonight, but Mr. Jacquard—he's not the sort of guy you piss off. He'll make sure you swing for something no matter what the evidence is."

"I would never hurt her," Jacob croaked, balling his own fists. "Never."

"Too late for that." He punctuated the statement with another right, this time across Jacob's face.

Jacob careened against his car. The security guard turned, walking away.

Getting into his car, he reached for the cell phone in his pocket. He dialed Mahjani's number.

"You're finished?" she asked without preamble. "Already?"

"I got interrupted." He shared the details, hissing slightly with pain . . . his jaw was going to bruise immensely. "What do we do now?"

Mahjani went quiet. He didn't know what was going on, until she finally sighed. "You opened the door," she said, her voice excited.

"I did?"

"You were possessed by Legba," she said. "He got some blood on her. We've got a window. We must complete the ritual tonight, in the dreamworld."

"All right," he said. "When and how?"

"Find someplace to sleep," she said. "A hotel, someplace you'll remain undisturbed. Then meet me and Rory on the island. I'll take care of the rest."

Chapter Ten

Rory waited by the ruins of the hotel. The sky was dark but clear, twinkling with stars, and the air was cool—although that might be the fact that she was naked.

"Hold up your arms a little higher," Mahjani instructed, kneeling in front of her. "I don't want you to smear these symbols I'm painting on your hips."

Rory did as she was told, looking straight ahead. She was strangely comfortable, being naked in front of Mahjani. After all, Mahjani had seen her in her most vulnerable state: having wild sex with Jacob, with Mahjani standing as mute witness. It was a little late to be embarrassed now. Especially not with what was going to be happening.

"You're going to be fine," Mahjani assured her.

"I know."

Jacob walked up next to her. He'd already stripped and

was walking stiffly, his cock flaccid. "I can't believe I'm doing this," he muttered.

"None of that," Mahjani scolded. "Stand still and let me paint you."

Rory watched as he stood, arms out, legs slightly parted, as Mahjani started to create the swirling patterns that represented the voodoo spirits she was calling. Jacob looked at her ruefully. She blew him a kiss, and his eyes glowed. She noticed his cock starting to harden.

"You two are amazing," Mahjani said good-naturedly. "I've never seen such an incredible amount of attraction. Or love, for that matter."

"I know," Rory breathed, feeling her chest expand with it. Mahjani finished with him, and Rory held out her arms. Jacob immediately headed to her.

"Don't smudge the paint!" Mahjani warned.

He kissed Rory, careful not to touch bodies. The heat and spark from the kiss alone was enough to have Rory shivering.

When they pulled apart, she realized it must have been a few minutes. In that time, Mahjani had created the ritual space, using a bag of cornmeal to sketch out another symbol on the ground. She was now drumming, a steady, pulsing rhythm. It sounded familiar.

Like Serafina's, Rory noted, and forced the wave of fear that came from that realization back down before it could debilitate her.

Slowly, she began to notice the loas materializing out of the very shadows surrounding them.

First, an old man, with twinkling eyes, hobbled in on a cane . . . then surprised them by tossing the cane aside, doing a sprightly dance step. He walked up to Jacob, and Rory held her breath.

"Papa Legba, guardian of the door between worlds, loa of fate," Mahjani intoned. "Thank you for joining our ritual."

"Back again, eh? Back again?" He patted Jacob's cheek. Jacob looked stunned. The old man then turned to Rory. "Pretty child. Papa would help you, blood or not. But you've your destiny, oh yes."

She didn't know what to make of that. He pinched her cheek, then danced next to Mahjani, clapping his hands in time with the drumming.

Next, there was a dark, handsome man, looking dapper in his white shirt with a black vest. He had a black hat and a pencil-thin mustache.

Mahjani kept drumming. "Greetings, Baron Samedi, guardian of the grave, lord of the dead," she intoned solemnly.

He tipped his hat, winking at Rory. Rory found herself smiling, even as Jacob took a protective step in front of her.

More loas came. The snakelike man, wearing a jacket patterned like a python's skin, moved in a strange, sinuous fashion. A woman walked beside him, wearing filmy rainbow garments. Mahjani identified them as Damballah, the serpent, and Ayida, his wife, the rainbow.

Then a warrior, a hugely muscled and incredibly handsome man, appeared, holding a two-edged sword. He wore only a loincloth. He looked at Rory with naked lust. Jacob glared at him. The man didn't even acknowledge him, taking a step closer to her.

Rory held her breath as the man studied her. He was gorgeous, mesmerizing. She tried to look away, but couldn't.

"This should be fun," he said, stroking her cheek. Jacob growled.

"No!" Mahjani's voice lashed out like a whip. "Jacob, don't touch him!"

Before the man could touch her further, a woman appeared in a beam of light. She was radiant. The sexual sway of her hips was as hypnotic as the man's masculine beauty. She was unbelievable. She walked up next to the man, removing his hand from Rory's cheek.

"Chango," she scolded lightly. He turned to her, smiling like a schoolboy caught in a prank. He then reached out, cupping the woman's buttock and giving it an inviting squeeze. She looked reproving, but Rory couldn't help but notice the woman didn't move away immediately.

"Chango and Oshun, lord warrior and lady of marriage," Mahjani said. "Now we are complete."

Rory turned to look at Jacob. He stared at Oshun. His cock was now fully erect, she noticed. She couldn't blame him. The couple were overwhelming.

The group of loas all took food from the table Mahjani had set up, "The feast" as she called it. Then they lined up around Mahjani, Rory, and Jacob, in a circle.

"Why do you call us?" Baron Samedi said. "What do you offer?"

Mahjani finally stopped drumming. She walked off toward the cave, bringing back a large goat on a tether.

"I can't watch this," Rory said, turning to Jacob. She buried her head against his shoulder, ignoring the squealing bleats of the animal as it was slaughtered. When it went silent again, she finally looked up.

"It is acceptable," Baron Samedi said, handing back a cup to Mahjani. Rory felt her stomach turn nauseously. "What do you ask from us?"

"Release this woman," Mahjani said, her tone supplicating. "She is held in this dream against her will. She needs to return to the world of waking . . . to the world of living. She has been at the crossroads too long."

Papa Legba nodded. "That seems acceptable."

Baron Samedi frowned. "Erzuli is holding her captive here, for the benefit of her priestess."

"Surely we're all as powerful as Erzuli," Chango scoffed.

"But do you want to be the one on her bad side?" Legba countered.

Chango laughed, a rough sound. "No, not me!"

Rory held Jacob's hand, her palm sweating. They were deciding her fate here.

"One measly goat hardly seems worth it, for something of this magnitude," the baron muttered. "What else do you offer?"

"They offer the ritual of joining," Mahjani replied.

"Sex." Chango smiled, licking his lips at Rory. "Of course. But the other, Serafina . . . she offers that, as well. All the time." He looked amused. "Even allows us to participate with her . . ."

"They offer love," Mahjani countered. "Theirs is a true bond, beyond fate."

This caused Oshun, the beautiful loa, to perk up, staring at the two of them with interest on her stunning features. She held Chango's arm. "That is different, husband," she murmured, her voice like the tones of a crystal harp.

"A suitable offering," Baron Samedi said reluctantly. "Let it begin, then."

Rory's stomach clenched. *Oh, please, let me go through with this.*

"What are we supposed to do?" Jacob asked quietly. From the tightness in his voice, Rory knew he was feeling as tense as she was.

"Just stand in the circle I've drawn, and dance," Mahjani said, her voice encouraging. "Close your eyes, and touch each other. Think of that night, in the cave. Think of your love." She smiled. "The spirits will do the rest."

The loas watched with expressions of boredom as Jacob and Rory entered the circle. Mahjani threw some herbs on a large bonfire, then lit it. The flames leaped toward the night sky. Then Mahjani began to play again, a rolling, hypnotic rhythm.

Jacob held out his hand to Rory. "Dance with me."

Smiling, she took his hand, then moved her body against his.

They swayed slowly, awkwardly at first, like a high school couple, a combustible mix of excitement and nerves. Slowly, the music tickled up through Rory's body like champagne bubbles, and she began to sway more naturally. She rocked her hips slightly. The beat was infectious. She closed her eyes, feeling the drumming wash over her in waves.

When she opened her eyes again, Jacob was swaying with her, staring at her. She danced close to him, her breasts brushing against his chest, his cock brushing against her stomach. His eyes lit with sensual fire. She danced around him, teasing him, caressing him with her hands. She brushed her hip against his, a seemingly accidental touch. He reached for her, his palm gliding over her as she swayed and moved.

Rory forced herself to focus on him, ignoring the slight movements of their "spirit" audience. Rory stared at the way the flickering firelight made Jacob's muscles stand out in relief; the way his eyes seemed to glow amber like whiskey in a crystal glass; the way his hands felt, hot and soothing and exciting against her already warm body. The night air suddenly turned sweltering. She felt a little dizzy.

Suddenly, she felt disoriented, as if she were viewing the scene from a place outside herself.

Jacob's eyes went low lidded. He started to dance with surprising grace, moving with hers in a complex series of steps that had their bodies pressing close together. Rory "watched" as she and Jacob started rubbing their hands over each other's bodies, smearing the paint that Mahjani had so carefully applied. They kissed, gently at first, their lips meeting then parting, tongues emerging to twine softly.

Her nipples were erect, dragging against the planes of his chest.

Rory remembered: focusing on every sensation, being one in the moment, she and Jacob had somehow created an amazing kind of energy. She relaxed, searching out the physical sensations. Slowly, she regained her senses, one by one. The rich taste of him kissing her led to the scent of him, musky and masculine, then to his touch, warm and rough and comforting. She reveled in each aspect, meshing herself more and more inextricably with the moment.

The dance turned distinctly sexual. Rory felt fire lick around her as Jacob stroked her breasts, cupping their fullness, gently circling and pinching the already hard nipples. She stared into his eyes.

She could tell the exact moment he, too, became fully present. He nodded in encouragement.

A burst of energy rose through her. She stroked the erect fullness of his cock, rubbing it against her stomach, her fingertips circling the shaft. She kissed him, her tongue stroking his as she gripped his cock between their pressed bodies. She felt the wetness on the tip, felt the springing tension as his muscles bunched eagerly. She felt her own wave of dampness, lubricating her body, slowly trickling between her thighs. She craved him inside her.

Their hips swiveled. Jacob hooked a hand over one of her legs, lifting it to rest over his hip. He reached between them, angling his cock, brushing it against her damp opening. She moaned out loud as the rounded tip pushed between her curls. He rubbed the blunt head firmly against her tight clitoris.

"Yes," she murmured, arching, standing on tiptoe, aching for a more complete joining as waves of pleasure rippled up from between her thighs. Her flesh tingled with desire.

Rory closed her eyes, focusing on the sensation of Jacob's penis, slowly pressing up and inside her cunt. She panted eagerly, holding onto his shoulders, lifting herself up against him. He helped her, putting his hands beneath her buttocks and positioning her so she could impale herself on his willing cock.

"Yes!" she cried out, her legs wrapping around his waist.

"STOP!"

Shocked, Rory turned her head.

Serafina was there, breasts naked, wearing only a filmy skirt. She held a long, wicked-looking knife in one hand, a bottle of raw rum in the other. The drumming stopped as she struck Mahjani hard with the bottle. Mahjani fell, bleeding from the side of her head. She didn't move.

"Mahjani!" Rory cried, as fear coursed through her system.

"I will not allow this!" Serafina pointed at Rory and Jacob with the knife.

"You can't interrupt, Erzuli," Oshun said caustically, sounding regal as a queen. "The ritual has started."

"Yeah, Erzuli," Chango drawled. "It was just starting to get good!"

"I built this world for my mambo, Serafina." The voice that emerged from Serafina's lips definitely sounded like a goddess . . . and a pissed one, at that. "This girl must stay here!"

"You can't control me," Rory protested.

Serafina-Erzuli laughed. "Do you really think wrapping your legs around some man is going to stop me?"

Jacob disengaged from Rory, and Rory felt an immediate sense of loss. The buildup of energy that she'd been experiencing drained away, like a bathtub emptying. Suddenly, she felt very small and vulnerable.

Jacob picked up one of the ceremonial knives, among Mahjani's ceremonial gear. He advanced toward Serafina, eyes narrowed.

"All right," he said sharply. "We'll finish this."

"You can't kill her!" Rory cried.

"She's right," Serafina said, amused. "As I said, I built this world. Kill me, and you kill her—and possibly even yourself."

"No," he said. "But I can *hurt* you."

Serafina's smile turned feral. "You can try." She opened her arms out wide.

He advanced on her. Rory stifled a scream, running desperately to Mahjani. "Please, help me!" Rory said.

"That one won't stir," Serafina commented, with an offhand gesture. "She's crossed me, and deserves her punishment. She will remain like that until I set her free or this world disappears."

Rory saw that Mahjani was, indeed, still asleep. Rory turned, and saw Jacob, just feet away from Serafina, knife held forward, eyes filled with dark intent.

Serafina laughed. Then she waved her hand.

Jacob's eyes widened.

"You don't belong here," Serafina said, shrugging. "So I don't have to hurt you. I just have to wake you up."

Then, just like that, he disappeared.

"Jacob!" Rory screamed.

Serafina crossed her arms. "Now, girlie," she murmured. "How to deal with you . . ."

Jacob woke in the strange hotel room. Blindly, he scrambled for his cell phone, hitting Mahjani's number. The third time her answering machine picked up, he realized that something was wrong.

She's crossed me, and deserves her punishment. She will remain like that until I set her free or this world disappears. . . .

Jacob closed his eyes. Mahjani was hurt, trapped. Like Rory, she was probably in some kind of comatose state.

Unlike Rory, she had no medical help.

Beyond that, Rory was in trouble. Serafina was not going to give her any options. Rory would either help Serafina, become her acolyte or Rory was probably going to become comatose in *two* worlds.

Jacob's mind raced. He turned on the light, staring at the bland interior of his hotel room. He had to do something.

But what, damn it? Even if I could go straight back to sleep, the woman will just send me right back here! And God knows what state Mahjani's in!

He closed his eyes, forcing himself to breathe deeply. He had dealt with medical crises before. He had worked long shifts in the ER, back in his residency, and handled life and death matters.

But this is the woman I love!

He had to get help. This was bigger than his pride.

Opening his cell phone again, he speed-dialed Aaron.

"Do you know what time it is?" Aaron asked groggily.

"No," Jacob said. "Shut up and listen to me. I need you to go to Mahjani's apartment, *right now*. I think she's hurt."

That got Aaron's attention. "Hurt? How?" He sounded completely awake and alert. Rustling sounds suggested he was pulling on some clothing.

"It's too hard to explain," Jacob said. "Just get over there, and if she's . . . well, if she's in a coma, make sure she gets to a hospital."

"Coma?" Aaron echoed, sounding shocked.

"There's no time!" Jacob said. "Just get over there. Break in if you have to, and make sure she gets help!"

"What about you?" Aaron said. "What the hell are you doing?"

"I've got my own problems." With that, Jacob hung up the phone.

He had to help Rory. The trick was to enter her world, and *stay* there.

He glanced at his medical bag. Then, like a puzzle piece finally falling into place, his mind clicked, merging data from her medical files, things that he'd researched about voodoo, things Mahjani had told him.

She remains in a coma so her dreamworld is sustained.

I am able to enter her dreamworld.

Therefore, if I am in a coma, I could remain there, as well.

He closed his eyes. It was a long shot, probably a stupid risk. But he couldn't think of what else to do.

He dialed Aaron back. "What?" Aaron barked.

"Listen, I have another favor—"

"What now? Jesus, this tears it. I'm having you fucking *committed,* do you understand? You've lost your fucking *mind!*"

"Yeah, I know," Jacob said. "That's not important right now. Take care of Mahjani." He took a deep breath. "And if I don't call you in twenty-four hours, I want you to come to this hotel." He rattled off the name and address.

"Hell. Why? You're going to be in a coma, too?"

"Probably not."

"Then what's the problem?"

"If I don't call you," he said, "it means I might be . . . well, dead."

A very long, shocked pause. Then Aaron finally found his voice. "What . . . the . . . *fuck?"*

"I'm hoping not," Jacob qualified. "I don't think it'll come to that. Just, please, make sure Mahjani's all right, Aaron. She might be my only chance if things don't work out as planned. Okay?"

Another pause. "Okay." Aaron sighed. "For you, Jake."

"Love you, bro," Jacob said, realizing he might not ever get another chance. "Oh, and the Lexus? It's yours."

"You're so fucking going in for psych eval," Aaron muttered, then hung up.

Jacob smiled, then shut off the phone. Then he opened his bag, pulling out a stash of various pills. He was lucky: he still had a little of what he needed left from an experiment he'd been running, before he took on Rory's case. *Gamma butyrolactone, 99+ percent.* Otherwise known as "G," a common enough street drug, he realized, pouring the crystalline powder into a glass. He poured water over it, swirling it around. Highly dangerous, the stuff was known to cause hallucinations, bradycardia, dizziness, weakness, even death.

He closed his eyes, then swallowed the mixture. With deliberate slowness, he put the glass back down, then climbed into bed, turning out the light.

Also used to self-induce comas.

Chapter Eleven

Rory stood, naked and alone, in front of Serafina. Mahjani lay in a crumpled heap on the ground. The spirits were standing around, looking slightly interested in what was going on, but not interested enough to help. Jacob was nowhere to be seen.

She was on her own.

Serafina shook her head, sighing. "When I entered this dreamworld, I never imagined you'd cause me so much trouble."

"Why?" Rory said, her voice shaking with rage. "Why did you do this to me?"

"Blame your parents," Serafina said easily. "They knew the bargain, and they broke the agreement. They consigned you here, not me."

"You told them that if they didn't hold up their end of the

deal, you'd put me in a coma and take over my mind and my dreams?" Rory asked in disbelief.

"Not in so many words." Serafina shrugged. "They disrespected me. They should have known I wasn't a woman to cross."

Rory clenched her hands in fists.

"Be angry with me, if you like," Serafina said. "But face facts: you can't be rid of me. If you agree to work with me, then I'll rebuild the hotel, give you anything you might desire. I'll give you a paradise."

"And if I don't 'work with you'?" Rory challenged.

Serafina's eyes sparkled dangerously, like the bright gaze of a snake. "Then I'll turn this island into a place that makes hell seem like a holiday."

Rory felt cold, not just from her nudity, but from the effect of Serafina's malicious promise, which seemed to make an arctic breeze pass over her. She gritted her teeth.

"What would you need from me?"

Serafina obviously thought her question meant she was buckling, and so she smiled smugly in response. "I can see now that you've got a lot of power, more power than I gave you credit for," Serafina said smoothly. "All I need you to do is join me. Learn vodun from me."

"Become a priestess?"

"Of sorts." Serafina's smile was broad—and lethal. "Help me with my rituals. Together, we'll be more powerful than anyone, alive or dead."

Rory's mind started to churn. "What are you doing rituals for, anyway? What's the purpose? You can't possibly have clients here."

Serafina's smile faltered, and her eyes narrowed to slits.

"She asks the loas for help in something they cannot give her," Oshun said, surprising Rory—and, apparently, Serafina, who snarled in shock. "Serafina wants immortality. When she has that, she will no longer need to stay imprisoned in your dreams."

The bonfire seemed to leap higher and wilder as Serafina's scowl deepened. Oshun looked coyly innocent, but did not back down from Serafina's foul mood. Serafina took a deep breath, then turned back to Rory. The smile she wore did not reach her eyes.

"So you see, it's in your best interest to help me," Serafina coaxed. "Once I get my desire, you will be free of me."

"You mean you'll kill me."

Serafina's eyes flashed.

"I'm not helping you."

Serafina growled low in her throat. "You'll do as I say," she said, taking a menacing step toward Rory.

"Or what?" Rory didn't back down, either, and out of the corner of her eye, she swore she saw Oshun smile. "You can't kill me here. You need me too much. If I die, you die."

"No." Serafina put out her hands. "But I can hurt you."

Rory's chin jutted forward. "I don't care."

"Aren't you acting brave, child?" Serafina's voice was mocking. "Funny, from a girl who's spent her whole life doing what everyone else told her to do. Why should this be any different?"

Rory stared at her. "What are you talking about?"

"You were a doormat! I've lived in your subconscious long enough to know," Serafina said with a sneer. "You chose the college your parents told you to. You never did anything without their consent. Everything you felt passionate about, they were scared of." She shook her head. "They actually thought they could outsmart me if they kept you in a safe little bubble, their privileged life. And you did everything they wanted, didn't you?"

Rory's throat constricted. She wanted to deny it, wanted to smack the smug grin from the woman's face. But a tiny voice in her head started to echo conversations from her past . . .

Don't touch that, Rory, you'll catch something!

Don't climb that, Rory, you might get hurt.

Mackie can't stay. He's too dangerous.

That boy's no good, Rory, he'll only get you in trouble; he only wants one thing . . .

Artists don't make any money, Rory, why don't you study business?

She closed her eyes.

She *had* been a doormat.

Serafina advanced, sensing weakness. "Your father, now, he was the hard one," Serafina said. "He knew, deep down, that he was wrong to betray me, but he was too arrogant and unwilling to lose face in front of his friends. So I made sure that the one thing he couldn't abide—his little girl, touching some man's prick—was exactly the thing that would cause his downfall." Serafina's laugh was like acid. "The one time you rebel, it lands you here!"

Rory felt tears start to well up in her eyes.

Had that been her life?

"Jacob said that I had simply accepted living here, on the island," Rory whispered, half to herself. "And . . . I did."

"Because you were used to submitting," Serafina said.

"Because there was nothing in my life I cared about going back to." Rory's voice was hoarse with regret. "I love my parents, but I hated the life I was living. And it took six years here, by myself, to figure that out."

She frowned.

It took six years . . . and one man.

She didn't have to settle. There was more to life, and she was finally willing to wake up and risk something.

"Do what you have to do," Rory said recklessly. "But shut up already. I'm tired of listening to you."

Suddenly, Rory felt a searing pain, like a knife thrust into her stomach. Gasping, she grasped at her abdomen.

Serafina bunched her hands, and the pain intensified. Rory fell to her knees, stifling a scream. Her lower back felt like it had been struck by a sledgehammer, and her stomach burned.

Serafina put her hands down, and like a switch, the pain disappeared, leaving Rory kneeling, with beads of sweat trickling from her temples. She felt nauseous from the remembered sensation.

"It's not so hard a choice, really," Serafina said dispassionately. "Help me, or endure pain. Now, what's it going to be?"

Rory grimaced.

"I'm . . . not . . . helping you."

Serafina's eyes widened. "You used to be so docile. What happened? You were such a *perfect* little girl."

"You don't know me," Rory said in a shaky voice, looking around for a weapon. But what good would a weapon do? What would hurt this woman?

"I know you," Serafina continued, starting to circle around Rory, her braids glowing red-tipped by the bonfire. "I *made* you."

Something clicked with Rory. "You did a ritual for my birth." When Serafina nodded, Rory smiled. "So the loas are responsible for my birth. I'm a child of the spirits."

The spirits assembled murmured something amongst themselves.

Serafina glared, and she quickly twisted her hands. Rory let out a short shriek before she could stop herself—the pain in her chest was a quick, sharp jab. "I was the channel."

"You were the order taker," Rory said, piercing Serafina's pride. "You were the middleman."

Serafina howled, looking more like an animal than a human. She raised her hands.

The pain engulfed Rory completely, and she did scream—a full-bodied, anguished cry. Her skin felt like it was scorching off of her bones. Razors of agony sliced through her.

Suddenly, it stopped. Shuddering, she looked up.

Serafina was lying on the ground. Jacob stood behind her, a heavy piece of wood in his hands.

Standing up on shaky legs, Rory whimpered, hobbling to him. He enveloped her in his arms, kissing her tenderly.

"*Shhh,*" he murmured. "Oh, Rory, I'm sorry I didn't get here sooner."

"It's fine," she said, clinging to him. "What are we going to do?"

He glanced down at Serafina. "I don't know. I'm going to have to fight her, I think."

"She could just send you away again."

"Not this time," he replied, with a smirk. "Now, I just have to—"

"That was fast." Serafina got up, blood trickling from her scalp. She seemed to grow, looming over the two of them, easily eight feet tall. "Took a tranquilizer, did you?"

"Something like that," he said, holding Rory tightly. "I'm not leaving her side again."

"Idiot," Serafina muttered, then waved her hand.

Jacob stood firm.

Serafina's face contorted with anger. "Wake!"

"Not gonna happen." His grin was challenging.

"Well, aren't you clever," Serafina drawled sourly. "Should have known a doctor would be able to put himself under."

Rory felt a chill of foreboding. "Jacob, what did you do?"

"It's all right," he whispered back, reassuring her.

"Is it?" Serafina asked. "After all, you've basically taken poison. You know that, don't you, doctor? Brave and chivalrous as it is for you to be here, you'll probably die, anyway?"

Rory gasped. "No! Jacob, is that . . . ?"

"You're worth it," he said. "You deserve the chance to live, Rory. And I love you."

"You could die!"

"My life was filled with case numbers and white papers before I met you," he breathed. "I never gave a damn about anyone, including myself, until you. If you don't wake up . . ." His eyes looked tortured. "Then I don't want to wake up, either. Because there's no point spending my life without you."

Rory's heart clenched in her chest. She swallowed convulsively, working the lump in her throat. "Jacob," she said softly.

"Touching," Serafina sneered. "Pointless, but touching. And exactly what did you hope to accomplish?"

"You're not going to hurt Rory," he said, pushing Rory back behind him and putting up his fists.

"*Hmmm.* You know, you're right. I'm not going to hurt Rory. In fact, I don't need to."

Rory's mouth dropped open in disbelief.

"I just have to hurt *you*, doctor." Serafina's eyes glowed with malicious triumph. "Then Rory will do whatever I say."

"I can't believe I'm doing this," Aaron muttered as he walked down the hallway of Mahjani's building. He was lucky she didn't have a doorman. He looked like hell, and coming up at this time of night had him looking like a burglar or murderer or something. He knocked on her door gingerly, conscious of the fact that the hallway had that palpable 3:00 a.m. kind of quiet, so empty that footsteps on carpet sounded thunderous.

There was no answer.

He knocked louder. "Mahjani?" he said. "It's Aaron. Open up, would you?"

Still nothing.

Mahjani was a light sleeper, he remembered. She would've heard the first knock. If she was on the other side of the door, she would have said something even if she hadn't wanted to open up.

He hadn't wanted to believe Jacob, but he'd felt compelled to do as he requested. Now, real anxiety started to course through his system. He pounded loudly. "Mahjani!"

After a minute, a neighbor opened the door. "Shut the fuck up, would you? I'm trying to sleep!"

Aaron muttered an apology, then waited for the door to close. Then he looked at Mahjani's door.

He needed to get in. He needed to make sure she was okay.

She slept with the window open, he remembered. He hurried back down to the door, then headed for the alley, pulling down the fire escape ladder. It descended with a clatter, and he winced, hoping the angry neighbor didn't have a gun. With adrenaline lancing through him, he shimmied up the ladder, making record time as he raced up toward Mahjani's floor.

Unfortunately, Mahjani's apartment was six stories up, and the fire escape wasn't actually at *her* window.

Gritting his teeth, he stared at the three-foot outcropping on the building's face. Lots of residents used it as a sort of shelf, putting potted plants or empty bottles out there. Her window was the third over, some twenty, twenty-five feet away.

He felt a gust of wind and gripped the railing, cursing Jacob under his breath. He pulled out his cell phone and tried her for the fifteenth time. "Mahjani, if you're there, pick up. Otherwise, I swear to God, I'm going in there to get you."

Still nothing. He snapped the phone shut with dread, staring at the ledge.

"It's probably nothing," he said to himself. "Jacob's crazy as a loon. Mahjani probably isn't even home. I'm going to get arrested for breaking and entering. *I am not falling six fucking stories just so Jacob can sleep easy tonight.*"

Of course, Jacob might be dead. And Jacob might be nuts, but strangely, he wasn't given to exaggeration. If anything, the guy tended to downplay disaster.

Face it. She's in trouble. You can tell.

He glanced at the ledge. She might be hurt.

She might be *dying.*

What if he were her only chance?

Taking a deep breath, he climbed over the railing, putting his foot on the concrete ledge. His balance felt unsteady, and he paused for a moment, getting his bearings. Slowly, he crept forward, his fingers gripping at the building's uneven brick face, looking for fingerholds. He didn't find any.

He swore as he had to step over some empty beer bottles, left outside a window. As he stepped over, his heel hit one, knocking it off. He tried not to watch as the thing hurtled toward the ground, shattering in the alley below. He swallowed hard.

Just keep moving. And like the movies say, don't look down.

Finally, he made it to Mahjani's window. It was open: she loved fresh air.

Of course, it was also winter. So it was only open a crack.

Grunting, cursing, he knelt down and immediately swayed. He grabbed the window frame, feeling dizzy, and held on until he regained his bearings. Carefully, he tugged at the window, praying that she didn't have some kind of stop or bar holding the thing shut.

She didn't. The window opened smoothly, and he tumbled in, falling on the floor with a loud thud. For a second, he simply lay there, breathing heavily, feeling an almost drunken sense of relief to be on solid land of sorts. "I hate heights," he muttered. "Jesus, Mahjani, I must love you to go through all this."

He froze. He hadn't meant to make the glib comment, but the moment it was out of his lips, he suddenly realized the truth of the statement.

He *did* love her.

Why else would she still haunt him, after a full year apart?

And what did he have to prove, to prevent him from actually admitting it—to her and to anyone else who might have something to say about it?

An expansive, light feeling burst through him, and he headed for her bedroom eagerly. He loved her. He could tell her . . .

He stepped into her room, and the feeling left abruptly.

There were tons of candles, votives in glass holders, all burned low and flickering. She was lying on her bed, fully dressed, her arms crossed over her chest, looking ceremonial. Regal.

Looking dead.

He rushed to her side. "Mahjani? Mahjani! Wake up!" He shook her lightly. "It's Aaron. Come on, honey, wake up. . . ."

Nothing.

He shook a little harder. Then he rubbed his knuckles up and down her breastbone. If she were pretending, there was no way she could ignore that discomfort.

Still no response.

He felt for her pulse. It was weak. Her breathing was shallow and uneven. Her skin was clammy.

She was in some kind of shock.

He grabbed the phone from her bedside, dialing 911 with fingers that trembled. "You've got to hurry," he jabbered, trying to warm her skin, trying to think of what to do. He was a doctor, goddammit! He could handle this. So why was he freezing up?

Because this isn't just some patient. This is the woman you love.

"What did she take?" the operator asked. "How long ago?"

"I don't know." He rattled off her symptoms, then waited by Mahjani's side.

The apartment was oppressively silent. "Mahjani," he whispered. "I'm here. I'm sorry I didn't believe you. I wish I could help you." He held her hands, stroked them between his. "I love you. It took me all this time—and a six-story ledge—to figure that out, but I don't care who knows it. I'm sorry I was such an asshole. I can't stand the idea of losing you."

If anything, her skin seemed cooler. He got on the bed, gathering her body against his chest, rocking her gently.

"Baby, I know how much your beliefs mean to you. I love that you're the kind of person who would risk her life to help someone in trouble. And if Jacob loves this Rory woman as much as I care about you—I can see now why he's doing what he's doing."

His throat rasped painfully, and he held Mahjani's still body tightly, as if willing his own heat and life into her lifeless form.

"Please don't leave me," he whispered. "I'll do anything."

It seemed to take forever for the ambulance to get there. When they arrived, they started taking her stats. "Do you know what she took? How long she's been like this?"

"No," Aaron said, feeling helpless. "No. I just found her this way maybe twenty minutes ago."

"Looks like she's gone into a coma," one EMT said starkly.

"Get her in the ambulance," the other replied, strapping her to the gurney.

"I'm going with you," Aaron said sharply.

"Relationship to the patient?" The EMT's question was probably standard, but Aaron still felt some scrutiny behind it.

Aaron closed his eyes. "I'm her husband," he heard himself say.

And, God willing, that will be true very soon.

Chapter Twelve

Serafina held her hands out, as if she were beckoning Jacob. He lowered his fists warily. She smiled, and he took an awkward step toward her. Sweat poured from his forehead, and he grimaced in pain.

"Maybe I don't even have to torture him," Serafina mused. "Perhaps I'll just have sex with him. Would you care to share, Rory? Would you want to watch what I would do to him? Would you want to see how much he'd *enjoy* it?"

Rory felt time slow to a crawl.

"Don't give in, Rory," Jacob ground out with obvious effort. He stumbled toward Serafina, two more awkward steps. "It doesn't matter what she does to me. I love you . . ."

Rory closed her eyes. She needed to think.

No.

She needed to *act*.

She picked up Mahjani's drum, beating on it slowly. Serafina laughed.

"What do you think you're doing? Going to play some music to accompany us? I like a fast beat," she said. By this time, Jacob had reached Serafina's side. She stroked her hand down his sweat-slick torso, then playfully nudged his cock, letting it bob. "Not bad at all. I'll enjoy this."

Rory focused on the drumming. The loas were listening. Serafina was too intent on her "torture," thinking she was going to exact some revenge on Rory by having sex with Jacob. She wasn't paying attention.

Rory had started the ritual.

Papa Legba hopped to her side, his ancient eyes alight. "We've had the feast," he said in a low voice. "But what do you have for an offering?"

She stopped drumming. Serafina was licking Jacob's neck, biting him. Rory picked up a knife.

Serafina laughed. "Go ahead and try it, little girl." She clenched one fist, and Jacob shuddered, going pale and clutching at his throat. "Come and get me with your little blade."

Rory held the knife high, looking at Papa Legba.

Then she cut her hand, deeply.

The pain was sharp but quick. Blood poured from her palm, into the cup on the ground.

Serafina immediately stopped laughing. "No!"

"I am the sacrifice," she said, holding out the cup to the loas. "I start the rite."

Serafina reached for her, releasing Jacob from his ghostly

chokehold. He fell to the ground, coughing painfully. "You cannot!"

Papa Legba stepped in front of Serafina. "I'm tired of your constant petitions," he said, taking a sip from the cup and smiling, his lips blood stained. "The offering passes."

Rory gripped her hand, then realized abruptly that the cut had sealed itself. Papa Legba winked at her as he passed the cup on. The other loas—Baron Samedi, Chango, Oshun, and the others—all took their own sips from the cup.

"What do you ask for?" Papa Legba said.

"I want to be free from this dreamworld," Rory said. "I want her cast out of my mind. I want my freedom."

"A valid request," Oshun stated.

Serafina stared at her with flat, hateful eyes. "I have made more sacrifices, and shared more power, than this child has in her entire life," she argued. "She's not even vodun. She's not initiated! She can't simply spill some blood—her *own* blood—and get your approval!"

"Serafina is correct," Baron Samedi intoned. "She is one of Erzuli's favorites. I don't want to cross Erzuli." He grinned. "She's the best lay in any world, for one thing."

Serafina's smile was beautiful and cruel as she walked seductively toward the Baron. "I can keep giving offerings," she said. "Have I not slaughtered and fed you on oxen and goats? Haven't I performed the sex rituals that have raised power for you? Surely, I deserve some favor for that!"

The loas murmured amongst themselves, and Rory felt a stab of desperation.

"She isn't offering you anything," Jacob said, in a hoarse voice.

Serafina hissed. Rory walked next to him, taking his hand.

"What do you mean?" Chango demanded.

"This is a dream," Jacob answered. "Her sacrifices, the sex, everything—it's all an illusion."

They all stared accusingly at Serafina. Serafina made a vicious gesture at Jacob.

Nothing happened.

"They are under my protection, Serafina," Oshun said placidly. "Until we sort this out."

Serafina screamed in impotent rage.

"What do you offer, then?" Oshun prompted.

Jacob looked at Rory, at a loss. "What do we offer?"

Rory closed her eyes. What did they have to offer?

"Love," she said slowly. She leaned against Jacob's comforting warmth. When she opened her eyes, the loas wore expressions of puzzlement. "You said you got power from Serafina's sex rituals. This will be even more powerful, because I am real, Jacob is real . . . and our love is . . ." She tilted her head up, searching for words to describe their relationship. His expression softened, and he kissed her gently. She turned back to Oshun, her eyes pleading.

"Your love is destined," Oshun replied, putting her hand on Chango's thigh. "That is powerful. Well, then, complete the ritual." Oshun turned to the other loas. "If they can offer us more power than Serafina, then I say we grant the request."

Serafina grimaced. She closed her eyes, muttering. Suddenly, the two pretty-boy men materialized, looking like gorgeous zombies. Another half-spoken word, and two men were suddenly "on," with the same ferocious sexual hunger Rory had seen before. "Let the battle begin, then," Serafina said.

Rory swallowed hard. She turned to Jacob. "I love you," she breathed.

He held her. "I love you, too."

For a second, all they did was hold each other, letting each other's warmth seep into the other as they embraced. Serafina was busy stripping off her clothes, stretching out with the men, starting to have sex with an almost comic frenzy. Jacob took his time, and Rory let him.

Just like in the cave, she thought. Be in the moment. Be present.

Be with Jacob.

It was as if they were all alone, making love for the first time. Nothing else mattered. There was no pressure, no stress, no outcome past this moment. He leaned his forehead against hers, his hands smoothing down her shoulders, stroking her arms. She pressed tiny hot kisses against his chest. She could feel the energetic connection between them, like a ribbon wrapping around them in a million little loops. He cupped her face with one hand, his mouth gently seducing hers with soft, probing kisses. She could taste him, rich and heady, like a dark Pinot Noir wine. Their tongues tangled and danced. She pressed her breasts against his chest, her hard nipples dragging across his stomach. He moved his free hand to one breast, cupping it firmly, squeezing gently. She gasped as the sensation rippled through her.

Serafina was riding one of the men while sucking on the other. It was a desperate, frantic mating. Rory's quick glimpse took in the fact that Serafina looked furious, distracted.

Rory decided to simply ignore Serafina, closing her eyes, pretending she was blindfolded in the cave once more. She felt the smooth firmness of Jacob's skin beneath her gently searching fingertips: the dip of his collarbone, the ripple of muscles in his pectorals and across his abdomen, the cut of muscle from his pelvis down to his cock. The springy pubic hair that covered his balls and lead to his smooth, hot shaft. The velvety blunt tip of his cock head. She smiled in delight as she fingered the tiny fissure at the tip, collecting the bead of moisture that formed there. She raised it to her lips, licking it with a tiny catlike lap.

He chuckled in response, then held her tight, his cock stroking against her. "I want you," he said, softly but urgently.

She nodded. "Then take me."

The flow of energy between them intensified. He laid her on the ground, kissing her breasts, the planes of her stomach, the flare of her hips. He stroked the spot he knew she liked, just beneath the moonlike curve of her buttocks where they met her thighs. Then he stretched out next to her. Reverently, he kissed her, long and hard, as his hand probed between her thighs. His finger parted the curls of her vagina, seeking out and finding the hard nubbin of pleasure that was her erect clit. He swirled around it with deft, increasing pressure. She gasped, her breathing going ragged and uneven in response. They continued kissing, deep, soulful kisses, as his hand worked on her pussy, now penetrating her with one finger as he stroked with his thumb. She moved her hips restlessly against him, and reached down to circle his cock with her palm. With her fingers, she gently stroked and pulled at his erection, feeling it pulse beneath her hand, growing harder and hotter. Soon, their kiss broke as they both struggled to breathe, their pulses racing, hips rocking toward each other as their hands worshiped each other's sex.

She was the one who broke. "I need you inside me," she whispered.

He needed no further prompting. He nudged her onto her back, parting her legs, positioning himself between them. Then, with one firm thrust, he entered her, filling her with his large, thick cock, burying himself in to his hips. She cried out. Then, the energy that she'd been sensing seemed to explode like an atom bomb.

The air around them seemed thick, florally fragrant, as shiny and iridescent as diamonds. It was alive with sexual energy. In a brief second of awareness, Rory realized that the baron was standing off to one side, as was Legba. But the couples—Damballah and Ayida, Chango and the beautiful Oshun—were instead giving in to the pulse of energy that Rory and Jacob were emitting. They seemed overtaken by it, helpless to reject the siren call of mating.

Jacob propped himself up on his arms, like a yogi master, his whole body taut and toned as he delved deeper inside her. She wrapped her legs around his, bringing him deeper inside her, rubbing her clit against his hard shaft, angling his cock head so it brushed against her sensitive inner spot. The pleasure intensified, and she started turning her head from side to side, overwhelmed with the sheer sensation of it.

When she looked to the left, she saw that Damballah had shed his python suit and was also naked, his body lithe and sinuous as any serpent's, but still human, and wonderfully seductive. Ayida had stripped off her silky rainbow-hued garments. Her body was full and generously curvy, her breasts heavy and tipped with rosy red nipples. Damballah lay on the ground, while Ayida sat in front of him, her legs parted, her back arched. His head was buried between her thighs, his hand clutching her hips as she writhed against him. She made slow moaning noises as he sucked and licked. Rory sensed that his snakelike features included an agile tongue, which he was obviously using to good advantage. Ayida gasped and ran her fingers through Damballah's hair, her hips bucking and gyrating against his face.

Turning her head to the right, Rory saw Chango and Oshun had succumbed, as well. Chango's loincloth was removed, revealing an impressively huge cock, dark purple with need, formidable as a spear. Oshun's body was sheer perfection, from hourglass waist to full breasts to long, curvy legs. He stretched out on the ground, beckoning to her. She straddled him, facing away from him, taking him in completely. He held her hips as she rode him like a stallion, her eyes closed, her breasts jutting forward and bobbing with each bouncing movement of their lovemaking. She let out a mewling cry of pleasure, rubbing her own clit, stroking his balls.

Rory suddenly felt a foreign wash of emotions.

It's the others, she realized with awe. She was feeling the sensations of the loas and their lovemaking, as well as her own. It was almost more than she could take: she could barely contain the emotions coursing through her body from the act of her making love to Jacob. She saw Jacob look at the other couples, as well. When he turned back to her, the hunger on his face was uncontainable, and she knew he was experiencing the same thing.

"Rory," he rasped.

"I want you to come inside me," she whispered, rocking beneath him, shimmying slightly so she could feel the hard heat of his cock against the inside walls of her pussy. "I want to feel you pumping in and out of my cunt . . ."

"Rory," He groaned. He kept her hips raised slightly, then lifted both legs against his chest, pulling her buttocks flush against his thighs. His cock was buried deep inside her, and he reached around her leg, rubbing his thumb expertly against her clit as he thrust powerfully, penetrating her deeper. She massaged her own breasts, the sensation of longing so powerful that she couldn't stand it. Then the orgasm hit her, shimmering through her like a wildfire.

Rory heard an echo of her own rapture come from Ayida, who had hit her own climax, thanks to Damballah's ravenous tongue. Then from Oshun, who threw her head back and let out a cry of joy as she shivered on Chango's eager cock. Rory watched as Damballah switched posi-

tions, entering Ayida and then leaning her back so their legs
were overlapping in a crossed position, like an open pair of
scissors. His cock was inside Ayida as she leaned back. They
looked almost motionless, except for the undulating motion
of their hips, pressing and withdrawing, moving with
serpentine grace against each other, bucking and raising,
then lowering. Chango and Oshun also changed positions,
this time turning Oshun so she was straddling Chango,
who sat upright. Her legs were wrapped around his waist,
his arms around hers, and they kissed passionately as she
moved up and down on his cock. He massaged her breasts,
his mouth open and working, their tongues meshing and
dueling fiercely as his cock and her pussy joined in hard,
deep, frantic contact.

Rory closed her eyes. The sounds of sex—the gasps,
the murmurs, the panting eagerness, the slap and slide of
flesh—permeated the air. She felt powerful from it, invin-
cible, somehow. All that mattered was pleasure, and she had
all the pleasure in the world. There was no shame, no pride,
no doubts or recriminations. Only here. Only Jacob.

Only love.

She wrapped her legs around his hips, pulling him even
deeper inside her, his hips snugly between her thighs, his
cock sheathed deep within her pussy. "I love you, Jacob,"
she whispered. "I want to take every inch of you into my
pussy; I want to feel your huge cock spurt, hot and deep,
inside me . . ."

He started to thrust inside her, with growing energy and
rhythm. She twisted her hips, her clit gaining friction and

sending shock waves of pleasure up and down her body. Her toes curled, and she gasped, angling her pelvis upward, pressing forward to meet him with every pulsing thrust.

"Baby, I'm going to come," he groaned against her throat, his hips moving like a jackhammer, fast and furious.

"Yes," she cried, as her own orgasm started to build, like the trembling precursors to an earthquake. Her nails clawed down his back as the sensation built to fever pitch. "Yes!"

"Rory!" he called out, his cock plunging into her, every muscle in his body tense as they shuddered together, clinging to each other, the waves of orgasm enveloping them completely.

The world seemed to explode. They were surrounded by a blinding light.

I love you, Rory, she heard in her mind.

Then everything—the island, the sky, the water—disappeared.

Jacob woke in a daze, his body feeling weak, his mind disoriented. He tried sitting up, then shook violently.

Rory.

He had to get to her. He didn't know what happened. Was she safe? Was she . . . awake? Had their "offering" been satisfactory, or was she now in the clutches of that vengeful bitch Serafina?

Despite the aftereffects of the "G," he forced himself to get up, drink some water. Weakly, he dialed Aaron's number.

Aaron answered on the first ring. "You're not dead, then."

"How's Mahjani?"

"She was in a coma, just like you said," Aaron responded. "She's still not—"

Jacob heard a voice in the background. "Are you Mahjani Rafallo's husband?"

"Yes, I am," Aaron responded, to Jacob's surprise. Then Aaron obviously muffled the cell phone with his hand. When he got back on the phone, Aaron sounded shocked. "She's awake."

"What? Mahjani's awake?"

"They said she just seemed to take a deep breath, then all her signs went back to normal." Aaron sounded mystified. "Jacob, what the hell's going on?"

"I can't explain."

"Don't have the time," Aaron pressed, "don't think I'll believe you, or don't really know?"

"All three."

"They're letting me in to see her now," Aaron said. "So if there's anything . . ."

"Can you let me talk to her?"

Aaron grumbled. There was another pause. Then the phone shifted. "Hello?" Mahjani's voice said, sounding a little weak.

"Mahjani!" Jacob said with relief. "You're all right? Does that mean Rory's all right, too?"

"I don't know." Now she sounded concerned. "I don't remember anything after Serafina struck me. What happened?"

Jacob relayed what he'd seen and experienced. She sounded shocked when he admitted he'd put himself in a coma. "That was very, very dangerous," she said sharply. "You should be dead!"

"But after what we did . . ." Jacob paused. "Is she all right?"

"I'm awake," Mahjani said. "I've been set free from that world, and Serafina's power. That tells me that Serafina is gone."

Jacob felt a wave of relief . . . until Mahjani's next statement.

"So either Serafina was banished or Rory is dead."

Jacob didn't wait for an answer. He hung up the phone, then left his room, hobbling as best he could to the front desk. The manager looked at him with concern. "Are you all right, sir?"

"I need a taxi," Jacob said, knowing he did not have the strength or focus to drive. "Right now."

Rory stood in a vast empty space. She seemed to have no body, no voice.

Where am I?

She heard Oshun's responding thought. *You're on the other side. In our world.*

"Am I . . . dead?" Rory ventured.

"Not exactly," Oshun replied. "You're at a way station. Your offering was more than we expected. Damballah and Ayida are still off somewhere, celebrating." She sounded amused. "Chango is snoring as we speak."

Rory smiled—at least, she thought she smiled. It felt like smiling. "Can I go back?"

"If you like." Oshun paused. "Serafina was right. You are blessed with amazing power. Your capacity for love makes you very, very strong. And, as you pointed out, in a way you are a child of the loas. You were created through our guidance. That means you are a part of us."

"Serafina," Rory remembered. "Is she . . . ?"

"She's dead."

Rory felt a wash of conflicting emotions, relief and regret.

"It was her time. Long past her time, in fact," Oshun said. "Baron Samedi is taking her to her new home. I think she'll find she feared it for nothing, so don't concern yourself. You have a more important decision to make."

"I do?"

"As I said, you are part of us, and powerful. You can decide to return as a mortal . . . or you can choose to join us, here, in this world. You can become a loa."

Rory felt shocked. "What does that mean?"

"You would be a spirit. You would have power. You could choose a mate, among the spirits. Even become married, like Chango and I. You would be immortal."

"What about Jacob?"

Oshun was quiet for a second. "He was brave," she admitted. "But he is, after all, still just a mortal."

Rory took a deep breath. "Then I want to return."

"It means you'll be a human," Oshun pointed out. "You'll be limited by the earth and its laws. You'll be mortal."

"I know."

"You'll die."

Rory felt a calm cover her. "I can live with that."

Oshun smiled. At least, it felt like she did.

"I thought you'd make that decision," Oshun said. "You'll live with my blessing. Both of you."

"So how do I get back?"

"It's simple . . ."

Rory felt something pull at her, an awkward, strange tug. Then the world went black.

"All you have to do is wake up, Rory. Just wake up."

Wake up . . .

Rory opened her eyes.

Chapter Thirteen

Jacob rung the bell at the Jacquard house repeatedly, then banged on the door. After long minutes, the housekeeper opened the door. He pushed his way past her, heading with painful determination up the stairs and down the hallway to Rory's room.

Mrs. Jacquard stood at the top of the stairs, in a night-gown and quilted robe, her hair in disarray. "Doctor White! Have you lost your mind?"

Mr. Jacquard was right behind her, also in pajamas and a robe. "I've called security," he warned. "You've got about two minutes until—"

"Rory," Jacob said sharply. "Is she all right?"

"Why wouldn't she be?" Mrs. Jacquard asked worriedly.

"What, did you think that when she lost your expert care, she'd die?" Mr. Jacquard said, stepping in front of Jacob in the hallway. His eyes lit with fury, his hands forming fists. "Take another step toward my daughter, and I'll—"

"I don't want to hurt you," Jacob said, gritting his teeth. His whole body was weak and racked with pain, but he kept moving forward. "But I'm going to see Rory, whether you want me to or not."

Carrie the night nurse came out in the hallway. Jacob thought that she, too, might be trying to stop him. Instead, she looked dazed. "Mr. Jacquard, I think you need to . . ."

Mr. Jacquard grabbed Jacob by the front of his shirt, shoving him back toward the stairs. If Jacob had been at his regular state of health, he never would have budged. Now, he buckled slightly, feeling the aftereffects of the drug like a hammer on his chest. He grunted, then grimly pushed forward.

Mr. Jacquard punched him. He took the hit, slamming against the wall. He glared at the older man. "You're an asshole, you know that?"

"You're trying to hurt my daughter!"

"You kept your daughter under your thumb," Jacob spat out. "And you treat your wife like shit. Hate me if you want, protect Rory if you think that's best, but if you hit me again I'm kicking your ass. I have to make sure Rory's all right. So shoot me, or get the hell out of my way."

Mr. Jacquard's mouth worked wordlessly, fury making him incapable of speech. He looked like a flopping fish.

Carrie turned to Mrs. Jacquard. "Really, you need to come see . . ."

Jacob stepped past all of them, limping into the familiar blue bedroom.

Rory sat up weakly, her luminescent gray eyes staring directly at him. She smiled.

"Jacob," she whispered.

He couldn't help himself. He fell to his knees at the side of her bed, weak with relief. "You're alive," he murmured.

She nodded. "So are you."

They didn't touch each other. A mere six inches between them, they stared at each other for a long moment, silently.

A ribbon of energy, thin but unbreakable, seemed to connect between them.

Then Mrs. Jacquard screamed. Jacob turned to see both Rory's parents standing in the room, with Carrie hovering behind them, in the door frame. They stared at their daughter in disbelief.

"Mom. Dad," Rory said, holding out a hand. Mrs. Jacquard flew to her daughter's side, her head on her shoulder, weeping uncontrollably. Mr. Jacquard simply froze, staring at her. "I missed you," Rory said, causing Mrs. Jacquard to sob even more loudly.

"Rory," Mr. Jacquard finally said, and the longing and sadness in the man's voice was enough to have Jacob reevaluate the man, at least a little. Losing his daughter had obviously torn him up. Having her restored to him might be the key to bringing back some of the humanity he'd lost. "Are you . . . you're really awake?"

She nodded, smiling, weakly patting her mother's head.

Mr. Jacquard turned to Jacob, looking lost. "Is she . . . is this . . . permanent?"

"I'd need to examine her," Jacob said, "but . . . I think she is."

"You knew that something had happened," Mr. Jacquard said. "You knew that something had changed. How did you know?"

"It doesn't matter, Mr. Jacquard."

"Dad," Rory interrupted, "Jacob saved my life. He's the one who brought me back."

"Jacob?" Mr. Jacquard sounded stunned. "He . . . how do you know him?"

She looked at Jacob. He shook his head, ever so slightly.

"He's my doctor," she replied.

Mr. Jacquard cleared his throat. "I misjudged you," he said slowly. "I've . . . made many mistakes. I haven't forgiven people."

Mrs. Jacquard looked up at this, her eyes tearstained and puffy.

"I . . . I just thought we'd lost her . . ."

Jacob nodded. "I understand. Let me check her over, do a few quick tests. Then you can spend all the time you want with her, all right?" He gestured to Mrs. Jacquard. "You two might want to spend a few minutes together. Things have changed. Perhaps you have more to talk about."

Mrs. Jacquard stood, looking hopeful.

Mr. Jacquard held out his hand. Taking a slow step, she moved toward him, accepting his peace offering. They moved out to the hallway, sending loving looks to their daughter. "We'll be right back," Mrs. Jacquard reassured her.

Carrie shut the door behind them, remaining in the room. "You did it, Doctor," she said, obviously impressed. "Whatever weird, crazy antics you might've used, whatever protocols you might've developed—it worked. You're going to be famous. The papers you can write on this case alone will—"

"Carrie, could you leave us alone for a moment, please?" Jacob said.

Her eyes widened. "What, alone with the patient?"

"Rory," he corrected sharply. "Her name is Rory. And yes, I'd like to speak with her alone."

Carrie looked offended. "It's not appropriate . . ."

"Just get out, will you?"

Sniffing indignantly, she left, shutting the door behind her with force.

Jacob turned to Rory. He still didn't touch her. It was as if he couldn't trust himself to. "Are you all right?" he asked quietly.

She nodded.

"And . . . are you going to stay . . ."

"Here? Awake?" She nodded again, her smile like liquid sunlight. "I'm not going anywhere, Jacob. This is my life now, and I'm living it."

"You have no idea how happy it makes me, hearing that."

Her eyes filled with longing. "We can be together now."

He sighed. "It's not that easy."

She looked pained, and it slashed at him. "What? Why not?"

"I'm your doctor," he reminded her gently. "There are rules. Ethics."

"*Screw* ethics," she said. "I love you!"

"I love you, too," he whispered. "But there are other things."

"What other things?" she demanded.

He wanted so much to hold her, reassure her. But suddenly, his conscience, logic, and rationality, everything he'd honed to a knife's edge in his years as a doctor, leaped to the fore.

"First of all, what would your parents say if I suddenly declared that I was not just your doctor, I was in love with you and we were together?"

"I don't care. I'm not living just to make them happy," she snapped. "I have my own life to live, and I'm not losing you because they won't approve!"

"It's not that. Like I said, I'm your doctor. If they think that I behaved . . . inappropriately," he said euphemistically, "with you, *while you were in a coma* . . . what would that look like?" He paused, waiting for that to sink in. "Criminal charges could be filed."

"You could go to *jail*?"

He nodded slowly.

"But we didn't . . . not for real."

"How would we explain that? How would they believe that your love for me is real?"

She blinked, at a loss. Then she frowned. "Fine. Then you stop being my doctor. In a few months, I'll get better, and we'll just . . ." She spluttered when he shook his head. "I'm an adult, damn it. I'm twenty, *er* . . . ," she paused, obviously calculating, "seven?"

"That's another thing." His logical mind had hijacked his emotions, continuing relentlessly. "You were just about to start your life. Now, you've fallen in love with me under very extreme circumstances. Don't you want to see what else is out there?"

"Nothing else out there is better than what I have with you."

His heart thrummed, resonating with the statement. He reached for her, stopping just short of her fingertips.

"You deserve a chance."

"*I'll* decide what I deserve."

He sighed. "At least think about it," he said softly.

"Don't you even *want* to be with me?"

He finally touched her, his hand brushing against her wrist. The heat of her branded his memory. He pulled away.

"I want to be with you," he murmured. "More than you'll ever know. And I love you. Which is why I'm trying so damned hard to make sure you're getting what you deserve."

She grimaced. "How long, before I can walk? Before I'm completely rehabilitated?"

He shrugged, surprised by her quick change of topic. Was she conceding that quickly, then? "I don't know," he said. "You were asleep for a long time. Your muscles are in remarkable shape, thanks to the voodoo I imagine, but . . . I don't know. If you're very lucky, I would say six months, working with a dedicated physical therapist . . ."

"Fine." Her eyes lit, like pearly gray beacons. "In six months, I will come to find you, Doctor Jacob White. In the meantime, you go do whatever it is you want to do. You won't be my doctor, we won't have any contact, no one will accuse you of anything." Her face was set with determination. "But in six months—*you're mine.*"

He smiled, his heart tightening. "God, how much I love you, Rory."

"Remember that, then," she said. "And I'll see you in six months."

"Mahjani, wait a minute."

Mahjani strode purposefully away from the hospital. "Aaron, just leave me alone."

"You're in no condition to go home by yourself," he argued, following her. She ignored him, trying to remember where the nearest subway station was. He put a hand on her arm. "Mahjani!"

She felt tears sting at her eyes. She stopped, turning to him, staring at his chest rather than his face. "I can't do this anymore."

He nudged her chin up, staring into her eyes. "Can't do what?"

"I can't keep letting myself hope," she whispered. "I can't keep hurting when you treat me badly, then walk away. I'm tired of it, and I deserve better. So leave me the hell alone, Aaron White. I'm finished with you."

He didn't let her go. Instead, he held on with both hands,

pulling her roughly against his chest. He kissed the top of her head, hugging her tightly.

"I'm sorry," he said, his voice rough with emotion. "I'm so damned sorry. I never meant to hurt you. I was an idiot."

"Yes," she agreed, trying to pull away from him. His grip was unbreakable. "But nothing's changed."

"I've changed," he said quietly.

Her eyes narrowed. Her heart started to beat faster—but hadn't she been down this path before? How many times was she going to fall for the same line, only to have him treat her like some kind of degenerate when voodoo came up?

No. She definitely deserved better, and she wasn't settling for less.

"Sell it to someone else . . ."

"I love you, Mahjani."

The words warmed her more than her wool coat ever could. She hugged him involuntarily, before pushing away. "I know you do," she said. "That doesn't change things."

"I know I was disloyal," he said urgently. "I should have stood up for you. I should have been prouder of loving such a wonderful, intelligent woman, rather than focusing on my embarrassment of her unorthodox beliefs. I have nothing to be embarrassed about. You are amazing, and I'd be the luckiest man alive if you agreed to be with me."

She blinked, causing the tears she was holding to trickle down her cheeks. "Nice words," she said. Then, carefully, she added, "They're easy to say."

He sighed. Then he released her.

Here we are again, she thought bitterly. *When caught in the clutch, he would always . . .*

He pulled out his cell phone, dialing a number. He placed his other hand on Mahjani's shoulder, keeping her in place. "Mom? It's Aaron. Yes, everything's all right. In fact, everything's wonderful. I'm going to ask a woman to marry me."

Mahjani's eyes widened, and she held her breath.

"Who is she? Her name is Mahjani Rafallo, and she's a professor over at NYU." He looked at Mahjani meaningfully. "She's also a practicing voodoo priestess."

Now Mahjani choked in surprise.

She heard the voice on Aaron's phone, jabbering quickly in an agitated tone. Aaron sighed. "No, I'm not joking, and no, I haven't lost my mind. She's wonderful, and I'm very in love with her. She makes me happier than I've ever felt." He paused. "No, she isn't one of my patients."

Mahjani let out a startled laugh.

"She isn't crazy, and neither am I," Aaron said, his voice firm. "No, I don't know when we're getting married. I still need to get her to say yes, actually."

Mahjani swallowed hard against the emotions clogging her throat. He released her, but she made no effort to walk away.

"Listen, Mom, I'll give you all the details later . . . yes, I know you wonder if this is entirely wise, and I'm . . . okay. Okay. You can send me an e-mail with your rationale for marriage criteria when you get out of your conference. In the meantime, will you let Dad know?" He rolled his eyes, and

Mahjani giggled. "Mom . . . Mom? Okay, I'm hanging up now. Good-bye."

He closed his phone, sighing. "That went better than I'd expected."

"You're going to ask me to marry you?"

He sent her a lopsided smile that had her heart melting. "Not a very romantic way to find out, huh? I was hoping to set up something more elaborate. I've got a carefully orchestrated scene set up at my apartment, actually. Roses, candles, champagne, the whole nine yards. But you wouldn't even talk to me." He stroked her cheek, and she rubbed against his palm like a cat. "I'd come close to losing you before. I couldn't stand losing you again."

He leaned down, kissing her tenderly, and she closed her eyes, giving in to the sensation of his firm lips brushing over hers with gentle, insistent pressure. She sighed against his mouth. "You didn't lose me last time," she couldn't help but point out. "You walked away."

"Yes, I did. But that's not what I was talking about," he corrected. "When I saw you in your apartment, lying in your bed, looking . . ." His voice shook, and he cleared his throat. "I thought you were dead."

She felt a shiver that owed nothing to the cold November weather, and hugged herself. He followed suit, wrapping his arms around her. "It was a close call," she admitted from the safety of his embrace. "I underestimated how dangerous the situation was. But Rory's alive, and awake. That's what matters." She tilted back, looking at him curiously. "So that's what changed your mind? The fact that my so-called imaginary beliefs nearly got me killed?" She shook her head. "Figures that it would take my near death to get you to understand how real my world is."

He grinned ruefully. "Actually, it had nothing to do with voodoo, or proving your beliefs. When Jacob called me and told me you were in trouble—that you might be hurt or worse—I lost it. I didn't want to believe him, but I couldn't risk it. So I broke into your apartment."

"Come to think of it . . . how *did* you get into my apartment?" she asked, surprised. "You gave back my key."

"I remembered you always keep your window open, no matter how cold it got." He shrugged.

Now she pushed away enough to get a good look at his face. "You broke in through my window?"

He nodded.

She shoved him. "Are you insane? Do you know how high that is? You could have gotten killed!" Residual fear and adrenaline started pumping through her bloodstream. She pictured him, on that tiny ledge, six stories up . . .

She smacked him on the arm.

"*Ouch!* Hey! I got to you, didn't I?"

She realized what she was doing and was abruptly contrite. "I see what you mean. The thought of you almost getting killed . . ." Her stomach twisted with anxiety. She let out a relieved exhalation. "Don't ever do that again."

"Well, don't go into a coma again, then," he replied. "I figured I was crazy, but I couldn't help myself. I had to get to you, make sure you were okay."

"So you couldn't talk to the building manager? Tell him you thought I was hurt, ask him to let you in?"

Aaron's eyes widened . . . then he looked very pale.

She stared at him in disbelief. Then, slowly, she started laughing. A few moments later, he joined in, laughing with her, shaking his head.

"I *am* an idiot," he replied. "All I could think of was getting to you."

"You must love me, then," she said.

"That's what I said." He smiled. "That's when I knew. Before, when I broke up with you, some part of my mind knew you were out there. I kept thinking, maybe things would change, or *you* would change, or my parents would finally accept me and get off my back. When I knew you might be dying, I realized none of that mattered. I couldn't wait for conditions to be perfect anymore. I didn't care about my reputation or even my own safety. Only you mattered."

She smiled, wiping at the corner of her eye with the back of her hand. "I love you, too, Aaron."

He put an arm around her, and they slowly walked to the parking garage, over to his car, a black Lexus. "I hope so," he said, "because I want you to spend the rest of your life with me."

"New car?"

He laughed. "New to me," he said. "Jacob gave it to me. A gift."

They got in. The leather was luxurious, the interior opulent. The parking garage was empty.

She felt a wave of desire engulf her as he sat next to her, smiling at her with love shining so brightly in his eyes. "I really do love you," she said.

"I love you, too."

"So . . ." She smiled mischievously. "How about we initiate this car of yours?"

"Here? Now?"

She leaned the car seat back, smiling in invitation.

"Are you sure you're well enough?"

"Only one way to find out." She licked her lips, feeling delightfully warm, wonderfully *alive*.

"Someone might see . . ." He sounded wary of the idea—but also aroused. His eyes lit with passion.

"Better hurry, then."

He smiled back, hungrily. Then he undid his pants, pushing down the fly and his boxers, letting his cock spring free.

She shimmied out of her panties and stockings, glad that she was wearing a long skirt. She scooted across the seat, straddling him as he leaned back. She kissed him ravenously, feeling his cock brush against the sensitive flesh of her inner thighs. He reached inside her coat, under her sweater, cupping her breasts, circling the nipples with his thumbs until she was breathless with arousal. She nudged his cock with her wet pussy. He fumbled under her skirt, positioning his cock at her entrance. She plunged downward, forcing him up inside her, filling her with one long stroke. They both gasped at the intensity of the pleasure . . . the incredible heat, in a world of cold.

She pushed her hips forward, feeing her clit rub against his pelvic bone and the insistent press of his cock inside the walls of her cunt. "Yes," she breathed, rocking back and forth, her buttocks clenching and releasing, her cunt squeezing around him.

He stared at her through low-lidded eyes, groaning, clutching her hips as she rocked and pressed. His hips arched upward, straining for an even deeper penetration. His legs were like boards, every muscle tensed like cords of steel. "God, yeah, baby, move like that," he muttered, his fingers digging into her flesh.

She threw her head back, breathing quickly, in short, choppy gasps. She bounced and moved, her breasts swaying. He leaned up, nibbling through the sweater, and she could feel the heat of his breath permeating the cloth. They kissed wildly as their sex merged and withdrew, pounding against each other.

The climax was close, she could feel the initial shimmers of sensation. She moved restlessly, picking up her pace, breathing quickly and harshly. "Yes . . . oh yes, Aaron . . . I'm going to come . . ."

He pulled at her hips, ramming inside her, and she muffled her scream of pleasure by biting his shoulder, yelling in ecstasy against the camel hair of his jacket. She felt his cock jump and pulse inside her, felt the hot spurt of his come against her pussy. They shuddered together, rubbing insistently, as if they were trying to mesh into one body of pleasure.

Minutes later, she collapsed limply against him. "I guess I'll let you take me home now," she murmured, nibbling at his jaw.

He smiled. "My home or yours?"

"Yours, I think," she said, climbing off him with effort and straightening her clothes. "I want to see this elaborate seduction scene you've set up. We shouldn't let it go to waste."

"Trust me . . . this was just an appetizer," he said, zipping up his pants and getting himself presentable. His eyes glowed with promise. "When we get to my house, I'm going to make love to you until sunrise."

"I'm looking forward to it," she answered, with a kiss.

Sunrise, she thought, as they pulled out of the garage and onto the road. *It was going to be a whole new day . . . and a whole new life.*

Chapter Fourteen

Six months later

"My name is Rory Jacquard. I'm here to see Jacob White."

The doorman at the desk looked at her with a kind smile. "Certainly. I'll call him and announce you."

"Please," she said firmly, as he picked up the phone. "I'd like to surprise him."

"I'm afraid it's against policy."

She stared at the man, sending him a winning smile. "It would mean a lot to me."

He smiled back, almost dazed . . . then cleared his throat. "I really shouldn't," he said, but it was a weak denial. "What if he isn't home?"

"I know he is." She turned up the smile a few watts, making

her expression winsome. "Would it be all right if I just went up?"

The man looked torn, phone still off the hook in his hand. Slowly, he placed the receiver back down in its cradle.

She beamed at him. "Thank you, Rodney," she said, reading his name tag.

"Thirtieth floor," he said, still looking bemused—as if he couldn't understand what had just happened. "*Er*, have a good day, miss."

She walked steadily to the elevator. *Thank you, Oshun.*

She'd progressed a lot in the past six months. Not just the physical rehabilitation, although that had been arduous. She had also spent a lot of time reflecting. The loas still visited her dreams now and then. They were her friends, her guardians.

She got the feeling she'd be learning a lot more about them in the future.

She rode the elevator up to the thirtieth floor, excitement pulsing through her bloodstream. Energy skittered through her, and she fidgeted restlessly, eager for release.

She'd been waiting for this day since the moment Jacob walked out of her room.

The doors opened, and she went directly to his apartment door, knocking without hesitation. When he didn't answer immediately, she knocked again, more insistently.

"All right, all right, I'm coming," she heard him growl. "But if it's you, Aaron, the answer's no. I'm not going back to work, and I don't want to go outside, so you might as well . . ."

The door opened. She gasped at the sight of him.

He looked exhausted. His blue eyes were haunted, smudged with shadows. He had a grizzled growth of beard that made him look less the smooth, suave professional doctor and more the rough male . . . more real. He wore an old faded T-shirt and a pair of jeans with one knee ripped out, obviously from exertion and not as fashion.

He looked good enough to eat.

"I told you I'd find you," she said, without preamble.

He didn't say anything. He simply reached out and grabbed her.

She wasn't sure what she was expecting, but it wasn't this. Nonetheless, she wasn't complaining. On the contrary, her body exulted in the feel of him, crushing his mouth against hers, his arms almost punishing her with the tightness of his embrace.

"Jesus, I've been losing my mind without you," he said, between kisses. He tore at her clothes, seams ripping in his haste.

"I've been getting ready for you," she responded breathlessly, shimmying out of her dress as he yanked off his shirt. She tore off her bra as he shrugged out of his pants, tripping on the band and falling over on his plush, overstuffed couch. He held her, and she tumbled with him, falling on top of him. "Why didn't you see me?"

"I couldn't." The words sounded torn from him, and his face looked tortured. "I wanted to, but I just . . . it *had* to be your choice. Do you understand?"

"I understand you're stubborn," she said, framing his face

with her hands. "And hardheaded. And I know I love you enough to overlook it."

"Thank God," he breathed fervently. His arms roamed her body hungrily, stroking her from shoulder to hip, caressing her breasts, her stomach, and the mound over her sex as he kissed her deeply. Everywhere he touched seemed to ignite with an exponentially growing desire.

She felt the hot rail of his cock, burning against her thigh. She moved restlessly, brushing against it with her pussy, moaning eagerly. He shifted, and she was beneath him, pressed into the deep cushions of his sofa. He kissed her neck, nibbling gently, then moved down to her breasts as his hand shot between them. He'd find her already wet: she'd started creaming for him as she headed for the elevator. Every thought of him brought a rain of wetness from her aching pussy, eager to lubricate the way for him.

Expertly, he stroked the tender lips of her vulva, circling the sensitive flesh, delving deeper to find her clit. When he found it, she cried out. "*Ahhh,* yes, right there . . ."

He pressed firmly, circling it, massaging it until ripples of electricity jolted up from her sex, up through her body, until her even her fingers and toes shivered with sexual excitement. She writhed beneath him, her back arching, her nipples jutting upward to drag against his chest. He groaned, then positioned his cock at her drenched entrance. When his cock head entered her tight passage, she took a deep breath.

He pressed in, and she gasped, a startled mix of pleasure and pain.

He froze. "Oh God."

"Don't stop," she begged, holding his chest. "Please."

"This is your first time, isn't it?"

She nodded wordlessly.

"Did I hurt you?"

"Only when you stopped," she murmured.

"I'll make it good for you," he rasped. Then he started to move, with slow, deliberate care, his cock withdrawing and pressing forward in long, loving strokes.

She closed her eyes, focusing on the sensations, dwelling in the moment. She breathed in the masculine scent of him, woodsy and yet still subtly sophisticated; she felt the hot firmness of his skin, pressing against hers so intimately. The way he so masterfully entered her, altering his angle by degrees, varying the depths of his penetration so that the pleasure generated slowly building and growing until she no longer felt pain, only an escalating fire of ecstasy that threatened to burn her alive. The plush, velvety luxury of the couch on her naked back and buttocks was a heavenly counterpoint to his overall hardness. She could hear him, his breathing heavy and harsh, his low moans and gasps of pleasure fueling her own mewling gasps of delight. She ground her hips against his, anchoring her legs against the couch so she could push her pelvis forward, taking him in deeper, meeting every thrust with her own matching pressure.

Suddenly, his lovemaking was less controlled, as she felt him get carried away by the tide of his own desire. It was as if all his masterful orchestration snapped under the pressure of his growing need. He was everywhere, devouring her mouth, suckling on her breasts, his hips moving in increasing speed and pressure, his cock pummeling her with frantic hunger. Her own desire exploded. She nipped at his lips, drew the edge of her teeth against the muscles of his chest as her nails clawed down his back. She gripped his hips, wrapping her legs around his waist to draw him in even deeper. She clutched at him, their sweat-slick bodies sliding against each other, molding and melding in an inferno of passion. There was no artistry, just sheer animal passion.

She felt the orgasm explode through her, and she screamed out his name, her cunt contracting against his hard cock like a vise. He groaned loudly, bucking against her. She felt the jerking of his organ inside her, felt the hot liquid of his release. The sensation triggered another orgasm, and his pounding cock hitting her special spot set off a domino effect of sexual aftershocks. Afterward, she trembled beneath him, her body weak and wrung out.

She felt floaty and weightless and wonderful.

He propped himself up on one arm. "Did I hurt you?" he asked again, his voice anguished.

"Not at all." She paused. "Did I hurt you?"

He looked startled, then he laughed. "I seem to be fine."

"Only one way to be sure," she said, stroking his chest. "And as soon as I catch my breath, I'm going to give you a thorough examination."

He nuzzled the hollow just behind her earlobe, and she sighed with satisfaction. "How have you been, Rory?" he asked softly. "I've thought about you every day."

"I've thought about you, too," she said seriously. "When I went through rehabilitation, the only thing that got me through it was thinking of you. Every step I took was a step that brought me closer to you."

He hugged her. "What else have you been doing?"

"I moved out of my parents' house," she said. "They were disappointed, but they understand. I need to live my own life now. I still love them, still see them. But I'm an adult now." She touched his lips with her fingertips, so firm, so smooth. "I'm still figuring out what I want to do, still getting used to the world. And I'm going to be studying more about voodoo. It's a part of my life, now."

He nodded. "Mahjani will help you, I'm sure."

She looked around. The apartment was technically clean, but still obviously in shambles. There were books piled everywhere, on a variety of topics. Voodoo figured prominently.

"Has she been helping you?" Rory asked.

He shook his head. "She's offered. But I've been studying by myself. It's been a way to keep me occupied."

"What about your practice?"

"I'm taking a break," he answered. "I don't need the money. I was driven by the challenge."

"And now . . . ?"

He stared at her, his heart in his eyes. "Now there are more important things to me than my career." He stroked a wayward strand of hair away from her face. "I want to spend some time getting to know you."

She smiled warmly, feeling love rush through her. "You'll have all the time you need."

* * *

A short time later, he scooped her up, carrying her to his bedroom. He placed her on his king-sized bed.

He stroked her back, easing any tension he found, checking for himself that she was all right. Her creamy honey-tinted skin was just as flawless and smooth as he remembered. He pressed hot, moist kisses down her spine, delighting in her shivers. His cock grew hard as he breathed in her sweet, exotic floral scent. He sucked the flesh of her hip, causing her to laugh. He caressed her sweet heart-shaped ass, tickling his finger down the cleft. Then he burrowed between her thighs, reaching for her inviting cunt.

She was already wet for him, a fact that only made his cock throb more insistently. He still drew out the exploration, stroking his fingers down her inner thighs, inhaling the scent of her arousal as he slid his palms down toward her calves. He kissed the sensitive flesh at the back of her knees. He wanted to know every inch of her.

"Jacob," she sighed, reaching for him. He stretched out next to her, reveling in the feel of her hot, soft palms caressing his chest, his stomach, the sensitive skin around his cock. She rubbed her smooth legs along his, her delicate feet tracing the line of his calf, her thigh resting on his hip. She stroked her stomach against his erection. They kissed again, deeper this time, tongues thrusting as their hips began to mimic the penetrating movements.

"I want you," she said, part plea, part demand.

He shifted her, pulling her to the edge of the bed so that her legs trailed off the side. Then he knelt next to the bed. He caressed the labia of her pussy, rubbing the mound over her clit until she was gasping and calling his name impatiently. Then he bent down, dipping his tongue into her well, searching her folds until he found the bump of her clitoris. Then he grazed the bump with his teeth, sucking hard when she gasped and pressing her thighs against his ears. He nuzzled and suckled until she was rocking her hips against him, then he pressed a finger inside her, high and forward.

She came, sitting up and crying out. He tasted the wetness of her release, and lapped at it.

His cock was painfully hard when he positioned himself between her thighs, making sure she was close enough to the edge of the bed to feel his deep thrusts right where she'd enjoy the most friction. He bent low, kissing her neck as he slowly penetrated her. His cock slid in without effort, lubricated by her orgasm, and he shuddered as he felt her hot, wet pussy clamping around him. He let out a shaky breath, then withdrew, then slid home even deeper.

They moved in a slow, sensual rhythm. She leaned forward, kissing him, even as her hips rocked and rose to meet his every thrust. He felt her hips moving, sexy and graceful as any dancer, swirling around his cock, altering the angle and depth of his penetration. She was breathing in short, choppy pants, signaling another orgasm. When she came, he was ready for her, keeping his strokes steady and firm. She cried out, bucking against his cock.

He smiled, then he withdrew, and shifted her position again. They moved to the center of the bed, lying side by side. He rested her leg on his hip. "You sure you're all right?"

She smiled. "I'm with you," she replied. "I'm perfect."

"You are perfect," he replied, sliding his cock back inside her pussy. Impatient, it strained forward, plunging inside her. He closed his eyes, struggling for control. "I'll spend the rest of my life wanting you."

"Don't hold back," she said. "I want you to come, Jacob. I don't need romancing anymore. I want you to *take me.*"

He growled in appreciation, then they started to move, bucking in earnest. His hips moved and flexed, entering her deeply as she wrapped herself around him. He plunged and retreated, moving deeper inside her as she clung to him, taking every heated inch. They slapped gently together with each joining, and the top of his shaft dragged against her clit, giving her friction to counterpoint with the steady pressure of his cock. He angled, aiming for her G-spot. He felt the climax building and strained to hold off, to prolong the excitement.

"Rory," he chanted, his hips moving faster, deeper, harder. "Rory . . ."

"I love the feeling of your cock," she murmured mindlessly. "I love the feel of you deep inside my pussy . . . *oh* . . . right *there* . . ."

"I love the way your snug pussy clamps around me," he answered, his voice hoarse with passion. "I love how wet you get, how fucking *hot* you are . . ."

Her head lolled back and forth as he plunged inside her.

"Yes, yes, *yes* . . . ," she called out, her nipples hard and ripe, her back arched like a cat's. "Yes!"

He felt the first shivering precursors of the orgasm, and he slammed home, burying himself inside her welcoming warmth. The power of his climax made him temporarily completely blank, a Zen state of bliss that he'd never felt before.

When he finally floated back to the bed, he realized he was still buried deep inside her. He nuzzled at the crook of her neck where it met her shoulder, and she kissed him eagerly.

A long time later, he rolled onto his back, carrying her with him, his cock still buried deep inside her. She nuzzled against him, her head tucked under his chin.

For the first time in six months, he felt truly alive.

"I love you," he said, his voice shaking with emotion.

She leaned up on her hands, staring into his eyes. "I love you, too, Jacob."

"I don't ever want to be without you again." The statement was a plea, and the naked vulnerability was frightening, but he pushed forward. "Live with me. Share my life."

Her smile was tender. She kissed him, slowly, and he felt energy pulse through them, merging between them, engulfing them in a radiating, shimmering world of light.

"You are my life, Jacob," she answered softly.

He held her tight. He might have woken her up, but he was the one who was truly awake now, thanks to her. He was looking forward to spending the rest of his days, and nights, with her.

CATHY YARDLEY has been entranced by fairy tales since she was three years old. Now, she spends her time weaving those fairy tales into modern retellings that keep the magic, romance, and twisted beauty in entirely contemporary settings and storylines. When not writing, Cathy spends time with her husband and son at home in southern California.